RETURN TO ADVENTURE

✻

John Creasey: a literary phenomenon. Author of more than five hundred books—more than anyone else alive or dead as far as the records show—he has written under ten different names. Nearly one hundred million copies of his books have been sold. They have been translated into twenty-eight languages.

Born in 1908, John Creasey has a home in Arizona, U.S.A., and a home in Wiltshire and he virtually commutes between the two. Married three times, he has three sons.

Apart from his home-to-home commuting, he has travelled extensively. Aside from writing, his great interest is politics. Founder of the *All Party Alliance*, a movement advocating government by the best men (and women) from all parties together with independents, he has fought four elections for his party.

Also in Arrow Books by John Creasey

John Creasey

Return to Adventure

ARROW BOOKS

ARROW BOOKS LTD
3 Fitzroy Square, London W1

AN IMPRINT OF THE HUTCHINSON GROUP

London Melbourne Sydney Auckland
Wellington Johannesburg Cape Town
and agencies throughout the world

First published by Hurst & Blackett Ltd 1943
under John Creasey's pen-name of Norman Deane
This revised first paperback edition
Arrow Books Ltd 1973

*Made and printed in Great Britain
by The Anchor Press Ltd,
Tiptree, Essex*

ISBN 0 09 906920 2

Contents

I

I Make a New Acquaintance

If you saw Cris walking towards you along a crowded street you would notice him whether he was wearing uniform or a tweed jacket and flannels. Not that he is particularly large or startlingly handsome; in fact if I were asked to describe him I would probably hesitate and then say vaguely:

'Well, he's a typical outdoor man, fairish complexion, blue eyes, quite a chin.'

You would get the impression that he is one of the countless good-looking, conventional young Englishmen who stream from the public schools and universities, paying far more attention to cricket and games in general than to business. If I happened to mention that he is comfortably heeled, even with income tax where it is, your impression would doubtless be strengthened.

In 1938 you might have been justified in your conclusions. I don't know, for he rarely talked about the era before the war, and I did not meet him until June 1940.

At that time I was wandering through France, heading towards the coast with a vague idea of getting a boat and rowing across the Channel, though I don't think that I seriously expected to escape from the holocaust. I was prepared to fall into Nazi hands, knowing that once they saw the papers in my coat, sewn inside the lining by a wrinkled, hard-hating Alsatian peasant only an hour before she was killed by a bomb, I was finished. The best I could hope for would be sudden death; the worst, a concentration camp. Without uniform as I was, there was no chance at all of my being treated as a prisoner of war.

I was a long way from happy on that interminable, straight road, with only low hedges and occasional trees to offer shelter. I was hungry and thirsty, and my shoes were worn to pieces, the soles tied to the uppers by pieces of string, when I saw Cris.

I like to think, now, that I know him more intimately than anyone else. His family would not agree, of course; I doubt very much whether Lady St. Clare approves of our association, for she blames me for the many risks Cris runs.

It was a scorching day when we met; the fierce sun leering down on the poor devils who were trying to get away from the holocaust of war. I had not had food or drink for twenty-four hours, crouching in a bomb-crater by day, travelling by night when there was slightly less risk, thanking God for the luminous compass I had taken from the body of a crashed Nazi pilot not far from Sedan.

I wore an old, tattered straw hat, picked up from the shambles in a by-road a few days before, and my clothes were so torn and dusty that most people would have taken me for a refugee. A native, I mean; I was a refugee all right.

My legs would hardly carry me when I saw a cottage a hundred yards away.

It was standing back from a road along which three giant tanks had rumbled twenty minutes before, so there was a risk that others would follow, or that lorry loads of infantry would soon begin to rumble in the wake of the tanks. But desperate as I was, I considered the risk worth taking.

I staggered across the untilled fields, the sun beating on my back, my tongue swollen and my hands trembling with the excitement of new hope.

The door of the cottage was leaning crookedly on one hinge, and there was no glass in the windows. Apart from that, the place appeared to have been little damaged. For the first time I thought that it might be occupied, but dismissed the thought as quickly as it had come. There were practically no occupied cottages in the line of the German advance. All but the bedridden had fled, to the fields and the woods if not in the hopeless trek towards the south along those corpse-strewn roads.

I went in, leaned against a bare-topped table for support, and stood quite still. It is hard to believe that one's whole body can be possessed with a vibrant ecstasy at the smell of food. Yet food I could smell, and something else too.

The odour was of burning oil. Both were coming from the room beyond.

The door was wide open, and I lurched across the floor, brought up suddenly by what I saw, or thought I saw.

For the room beyond was crammed with pictures and oleographs, sepia-coloured portraits and little ornaments. On a square table in the middle of the room was a green chenille tablecloth, and, on that, a vase of tulips.

A brazier was set beneath the wide chimney, and above it was a hook. Both brazier and hook were empty, but in one corner of the fireplace was an oil-stove showing a blue flame. Above the stove was a saucepan, and from the saucepan steam was rising about the edges of the lid.

I stretched out a hand, and would have touched it but for a man's voice behind me, startling me, making me swing round with a belated surge of alarm, close to terror.

'*Bonjour, M'sieu*,' said the speaker gravely.

Standing on the threshold of the door which I had just entered was Cris, although I did not know then that that was his name.

He was dressed in R.A.F. uniform, tattered, but unmistakable.

Absurdly, I answered: '*Bonjour, M'sieu*.'

My tongue, which had been silent for days and might have been expected to refuse to work except with an effort, ran away with me, for by habit and training I am a cautious, uncommunicative kind of fellow, believing it wise to let the other man talk first.

I told him I was hungry and thirsty but I had not intended to rob him, I wanted to know whether he had seen any Nazis. And: was there anyone else at the cottage, how long had he been here, what was in the stewpan, was there any water, was he sure the well was safe, a lot had been poisoned, did he know that? I went on and on in a kind of babbling daze, staring at the doorway.

No, there was no one there. It had been an apparition, a mirage. I groaned and pressed my fingers against my forehead, closing my eyes. I suppose I stayed like that for several minutes, and that the shock had robbed me of any kind of feeling, for I did not start when he touched my shoulder and said easily:

'The water's all right, I've boiled it in case of accidents. Easy, now, don't take it all at once!'

My hands moved from my face and I made a convulsive movement towards the water, but he held a tin mug so that I could only sip a little at a time.

'Take a mouthful and hold it in your mouth for a few seconds, you'll get full benefit then.' He spoke quietly, as if to a feverish child. I obeyed him, and the water soaked itself into my parched tongue and raw cheeks and lips. Only then did he let me drink again.

'You can have some more if you lean back and close your eyes for five minutes,' he said. 'Do you think you can manage it?'

I kept my eyes closed, not with any great effort. I have known the bite of rye whisky in my veins, but never a spirit with an effect equal to that one mug of boiled water.

'Good man, the five minutes is up. Think you can manage the spoon?'

He was holding a basin towards me; the smell alone was enough to set me trembling. I seized the spoon he offered, and this time he did not try to curb me, calmly setting the table for two, folding back the green cloth and taking knives and forks from the drawer in the table. Out of the saucepan he took a chicken. I stared at it eagerly although the first pangs of hunger were satisfied, and I had patience enough to wait until he brought half a loaf of coarse brown bread. Soberly he cut two slices, not over-thick, put one by the side of each plate, and then looked down on the chicken contemplatively.

'You can't carve, I suppose?'

'Carve?' I choked. 'Don't worry about that. Pull it apart!'

'Practical, but a bit messy,' he said. Methodically he came to grips with the chicken, then took a clean handkerchief from his pocket. This he lay over the remainder of the bird.

'That'll serve as a meat-cover,' he said. 'Let's weigh in. It's the first chicken I've had for a long time.'

Neither of us spoke. He ate slowly, relishing each morsel and breaking his bread carefully. I followed his example, by then feeling somewhat ashamed of my past exhibition. He made no comment until it was over, then went into the other room, to return with two mugs filled with water.

'They forgot to leave any coffee,' he said, and eyed the bones on our plates thoughtfully. 'Yes, my first chicken for a long time. The first one I've ever killed, too. You'd think after the last week that wringing a chicken's neck would be easy,' he reflected, 'but I'm damned if I didn't feel queasy. You don't happen to have a cigarette, do you?'

'Cigarette?' I said, and drew out of my tattered pocket a case holding eight cigarettes. I proffered them with a certain pride.

'Good Lord!' he said. 'This is a miracle! I've a match.'

'If there are any miracles about, you've provided them,' I said. 'I'd given up hoping for food unless they gave me some.'

He did not ask who I meant by 'they', but answered quietly: 'Not likely.'

He stared at and beyond me, as if gazing into some unfathomable distance. It was an expression I was to know well, but then it awed me, rather.

The pause grew over-long, and I said awkwardly: 'How long have you been here?'

He came back to earth with a start.

'Eh? I'm sorry, I didn't hear you.'

'I asked how long you've been here,' said I. 'Not that it matters a hoot, it was just something to say.'

He smiled. 'About three days, I suppose. Had to lay up. Have you ever wanted to kill yourself because you were so damnably useless? Have you ever—but it doesn't matter.' He pushed his chair back. 'You look all in, you'd better have some sleep.'

I murmured something about being all right, but he made me get up and extinguish my cigarette, then led me out of the cottage to a small barn. How he helped me up the ladder to the loft I don't know. I remember a vague impression of stumbling over masses of straw, stretching my racked body out, and falling asleep.

It was dark when I woke up.

The heaviness of my sleep was proved by the fact that although I heard sounds I did not immediately recognise them, despite the dozen times in the past week when I had cowered in stark fear at the sound of German voices, the movement of equipment and the stamping of military feet.

The first recognisable sound came from my side, and with it a hand was put over my mouth.

'Keep quiet.' The voice was a whisper, but I heard it and in a moment full realisation of what had happened came to me. I went rigid enough for Cris to remove his hand. He went on: 'We're getting out of here. Follow me.'

We moved silently across the loft. I did not see how we could get out before the men entered the barn, but I need not have worried, for he led me to a gap in the boarding through which I saw a pale red glow in the skies, and further away the white burst of a shell.

With infinite caution, Cris manœuvred a ladder into position. Even so, he could not avoid making some noise, and every moment I expected to hear a harsh challenge. Footsteps were actually approaching the barn from the cottage when eventually I scrambled down the ladder after him. Once landed, he gripped my arm again and led me across the yard to a field.

The movement of the troops behind us was growing noisier. An officer was bellowing orders, while a car drew up, its headlamps illuminating the road. I crept on in deadly fear, expecting every moment to hear a shout of recognition. But none came, and soon we were some thirty or forty yards from the cottage. This distance seemed to content Cris, but I was impatient to put more ground between us and the enemy.

'Don't worry,' he whispered. 'They won't come after us. Just keep your head down and wait. This is going to be worth seeing.'

2

I Learn to Respect and Admire

I was frightened; but I was also puzzled. Cris's attitude appeared to me to be suicidal. Yet I could not go forward on my own, and in any case his last sentence re-echoed in my mind.

'*This is going to be worth seeing.*'

Some thirty seconds passed before I asked: 'What the devil do you mean?'

'Head down!' urged Cris. 'It's due now.'

Automatically I covered my ears with my hands. I had no idea where the explosion he obviously expected was coming from, but I knew grim earnestness when I heard it.

The flash hurled itself against my eyes, and quickly after it came the explosion. The blast lifted me a foot from the ground, and I heard the hiss of metal hurtling through the air. In itself it was not frightening; it was one of the things I had grown used to. But the mystery of it, the unknown factor which is always more scarifying than known fact, made me jumpy and nervous.

In the glow of the ensuing fire I saw Cris staring beyond the hedge towards the cottage; or what had been the cottage. His face was set and quite expressionless, but there was a queer air of satisfaction about him.

There was little of cottage or barn standing. The former was a shell, on fire, and pieces of burning debris, probably hay from the barn which no longer existed as a recognisable unit, were dotted over a wide area, adding to the garish light. I saw half a dozen uniformed Nazis staggering away from the flames, while others lay quite still. The car was on its side, wheels gaping towards us.

'That's a dozen of the swine who won't do any more damage,' said Cris quietly.

He turned to lead the way, walking swiftly, almost too swiftly for me, although I managed to keep up with him. The ground was fairly even, and gave us little trouble, so that in half an hour we had travelled some two miles.

We crossed the road. There was no traffic on it, although in a ditch on the far side I stumbled against something.

It was a woman's body.

'What's keeping you?' Cris demanded, and looked down at me. I heard the sharp intake of his breath, and there was a savage note in his voice as he added: 'Come on, we haven't time to waste.'

I scrambled up and followed him, wondering whether he knew where he was going.

'I've an illuminated compass which might be useful,' I ventured at last.

'A compass?' Cris asked, and turned to look at me.

'One way and the other, you were a find,' he added. He said nothing more till we had reached a clump of trees and were safely beneath their branches.

There was a well-defined path, but he did not take it, walking alongside very cautiously. I fancied that I heard sounds; if I did they were no more than the creatures of the night stirring, perhaps already awake because of the strange violence that had come on earth.

'Safe enough, I think,' Cris said then, 'and that much nearer to our salvation.'

'And that is?'

Cris chuckled. 'Wait until you've seen her.'

I suppose such hints and reticences could have been irritating; but in truth my mind was still reeling from the nearness of disaster, and the destruction of the cottage.

We broke through the trees into a clearing.

'It's a ring,' Cris said. 'By the grace of God and the light of a flare I managed to land in the middle of it, and there wasn't much damage done. There's enough in her tank to get us to the other side.' He stared into the darkness, which only slowly resolved itself into the shape of an aeroplane. My heart was beating so fast that I could hardly control myself. 'Good old Sal,' Cris addressed it affectionately. 'Talking of names, what's yours?'

'Deane,' I said, without thinking.

'I'm St. Clare,' he said. 'Cris would probably be easier. What do you get called?'

I stared at the vague blur of his face, hearing the laughter in his voice but not quite able to comprehend it. Perhaps he was amused, as I grew to be, by the fact that we were standing in a copse in a country overrun with our enemies, discussing names.

'Called? Well, Norman . . .'

'Lord, that won't do!' Cris exclaimed. 'Let's plump for Ned. I suppose we ought to get some more sleep, we can't do much until the morning.'

'I'm not tired,' I said, and meant it.

'Good,' said Cris promptly. 'I am. You take first watch, but don't let me sleep more than a couple of hours.' He handed me his wrist-watch, the ghostly hands of which pointed to half past three. 'That'll be near enough to dawn,' he added, falling like a stone into the long grass.

'My God!' I remember saying aloud. 'He's asleep.'

I stood staring down at him, respect and admiration growing in me for Crispian St. Clare.

Until then I had not been conscious of any emotion but gratitude and relief, but now, reviewing the suddenness with which he had fallen asleep, they burgeoned into something deeper; for it proved the degree of his fatigue. While I had been sleeping, and later feeling sorry for myself, he had been ready to drop. But I swear no one could have discerned it in his manner or his voice.

It was very quiet except for the distant sounds of gun-fire and bombing, and the occasional hum of an engine overhead. For the first time I thought of the machine up there dispassionately, and not as an angel of destruction seeking me out. Once I saw a pair of green eyes peering at me from the undergrowth. I made no sound, and did not move; the eyes disappeared, and my heart beat more steadily.

Listening to Cris's even breathing, I no longer felt hunted and alone. I found my mind working with the quietness and precision which years of training had inculcated in me.

That night it did not seem too long since I had first entered the Foreign Office as a young man whose chief asset was a knowledge of foreign languages. In those days

17

I was more politically inclined, and like many youngsters of twenty-two felt that the burden of putting the world to rights rested entirely on my shoulders. I went into the Foreign Office because my father had been there and had contrived to pull the necessary strings.

At first I had rebelled against obtaining a position by influence and accident of birth, but a talk with my father had sobered me. It was in 1930, in the depth of the depression, and although he had a good pension, things had not gone well with him, while for years my mother's poor state of health had strained the family exchequer.

On that June night, with the noises of war in my ears, I could hear myself saying:

'You've been more than good, Dad, but I can't go into this. Can't you see that the Government's all wrong?'

'Let's not generalise,' my father said mildly. 'This is personal and particular to us, Norman. If you think you can make a living while maintaining these ideas, go on with it. But it isn't easy, and it won't be any easier. You've been used to a soft life. I suppose you realise that?'

It was one of the things with which I often reproached myself; certainly I realised it. I was about to say so when I had a quick, unbidden thought.

'Dad—how badly have you been hit, financially?'

'That isn't the point,' he began, and after a while he admitted that he was concerned with what would happen to my mother if he died and his pension died with him. He would go no further than that, and the talk finished inconclusively, but I wondered why he should be so perturbed, for he was no more than sixty-three and there was nothing to indicate that he would not be hale and hearty for another ten years.

I called to see McPherson, our family doctor, the next

day. There I took it as hard as I could, and as straight and direct as the old Scotsman could give it to me. My father would not live another twelve months, perhaps not six.

Of course, I joined the Foreign Office, and began to learn how to be discreet.

I was not looked upon with any favour by my contemporaries for some time, but I had too much to worry about at home to be concerned with that. My father died, eight months later. The salary of a member of the F.O. staff is not big; in fact I needed a supplementary income to put up a show in common with my acquaintances. There was no chance of putting up the show, but I do not think my mother felt the consequences of the financial depression.

When she died, in 1938, I was too far immersed in the F.O. to get out of it, or to want to. Much of my work had taken me to Berlin. I liked neither what I saw nor what I heard, and said so cautiously. Not cautiously enough, as it turned out, for I was sent to South America in the early weeks of 1939, but recalled hurriedly in June for 'special work' in Germany.

I had been asked by Sir Alan Clyde, the Foreign Office political adviser, to collect some papers from the Embassy in Berlin, and was out of the capital with them just before the war started. Then I was sent into Alsace, for work with the French. I was worried and apprehensive about the French; there were far too many different ideas for my liking, far too much sympathy with Nazi-ism as a creed, particularly amongst some of the officers. I said so in my reports, and was directed to contact in Metz one of the Secret Intelligence men collecting information about the reliability or otherwise of high members of the French General Staff. To this day I have never known why Metz was the rendezvous, but I met my man and received the papers.

He was murdered two hours later; and I began my journey across France with those papers sewn in my pocket. I was heading for Paris, with St. Dizier my first town *en route*. Afterwards I was driven north-west, but the last time I had been able to check my whereabouts I had been near Rheims. From there I had travelled nearly due west for the coast.

The importance of the papers could hardly be estimated; the Secret Intelligence man had emphasised that strongly enough, and his murder proved it to my satisfaction.

There is little point in telling again of the tragedy of the breakthrough at Sedan, the murder of refugees, the blasting of whole towns out of existence, the grim, enraging story of the French unpreparedness and lack of heart, the latter only amongst the people in high places, for the peasants hated the Nazis as thoroughly as they hate the name of Germany. I travelled through that slough of blood and misery buoyed up by the thought that we, the British, *were* fighting all we knew, for I had seen a thousand times the toughness and the recklessness of our fighter and bomber squadrons; and little dreamt of our own unpreparedness at home.

That is what had happened to me, before I met Cris.

That early morning, in a strange mood of elation, with no awareness of fear, with the past vivid in my mind and hope for the morrow higher than I had known it for a week and more, I walked about the clearing and about 'Old Sal', hearing Cris breathing steadily whenever I neared him.

Dawn was coming as the two hours approached.

I knew the importance of being precisely on time, and

awakened Cris exactly two hours after he had gone to sleep.

My hand touched his shoulder, and he awakened at once. For a moment I was startled; his expression was grim to a point of being forbidding.

Then he gave the crooked smile I was beginning to expect.

'Hello, Ned,' he said. 'How are things?'

'Nothing to report, sir. I'm sorry the milk hasn't arrived, and I can't make the tea yet.'

Cris grinned.

'If you're asking for a drink of water, there's a bottle or two in Sal. And the chicken and bread's in my respirator case.' He stood up and stretched himself, while I hurried to the machine, a gaunt sight in the growing light. I wondered what had happened to the rest of the crew.

The water was cool and welcome, the food satisfying. I reasoned that in three hours we could be in London, once Sal was in the air.

Cris went inside the cabin, saying as he did so: 'It needs a couple of hours' work, Ned, and we'll be ready to take off. I thought I'd get it done yesterday, but it didn't work out.'

I checked abruptly, realising that he had worried about me instead of using his precious time to get the machine airworthy. I covered my feelings by asking how he had known that the cottage would be blown up the previous night.

He stared at me.

'Good Lord, hasn't that sunk in? I landed with a full bomb-rack of 100-pounders, lugged 'em over to the cottage and placed 'em in position, set to bounce when we were safely away.'

I gasped; I had a sudden picture of him carrying the bombs one by one to the cottage, planning his trap for the moment the Nazis took it over.

'Come on, shake out of it,' said Cris. 'You're not a first-class mechanic, are you? . . . No, I thought you wouldn't be. But you've got the compass, and the cigarettes, and you can hold things for me while I fiddle.' He turned cheerfully to one of the engines, the cowl of which was only loosely screwed down.

I held odds and ends, and watched the sky lightening, saw the little silvery shapes high in the heavens, heard the barking of ack-ack guns not far away, and soon the inevitable medley of crumps from the bombs.

'I wonder where they are today?' Cris said. 'You get hardened to it, don't you?'

I knew that he was not hardened any more than I, but I nodded, while he worked and the sun rose over the tops of the trees.

I do not know how long I had been standing there when I saw the movement. I happened to glance over my shoulder, and probably had heard a faint sound. As it was I saw the figure of a man hiding in the trees, and the sight sent a shock through me which momentarily paralysed my voice.

'We're being watched,' I quavered. 'Fellow over . . .'

I went no further, for the man broke cover and there were several others behind him. I turned to see the leader pointing a revolver towards us. My heart turned over, while Cris moved round with a spanner in one hand and a smear of grease on his right cheek.

22

3

I Report a Success

I had given up trying to understand my reactions and mental processes during the few hours immediately following my meeting with Cris. I know that as I stared at the little party of uniformed men I believed them to be hostile, although they were in French uniform, bedraggled and exhausted, unshaven and grim. Perhaps it was their appearance which consolidated the fears first born in me when I had glimpsed the movement without recognising the uniforms.

I can recall the hunted horrors of the week before I saw the cottage, and the things I had seen; they hardly bear repeating, for I had passed through a dozen towns so devastated that 'no brick stood on brick' was barely an exaggeration. Most of those French towns had been crowded with refugees, and three times I had crouched amongst the dropping bombs, shaken and yet paralysed with sharp personal fear. After a while the instinct of self-preservation grew less dominant. I must have dragged a dozen, no, many more, women and old men from acute danger. I do not think the risk, *my* risk, ever occurred to me, for I acted instinctively; but when I returned to the pitiful shelter I had found for myself I would shake like a man in a bout of malaria. But this is less a book about myself than about Cris, and there is no doubt at all that his leadership and serene optimism had a considerable influence on me.

During the night I had experienced a complete divorcement from my past experiences. I was in the ring of trees, cut off from observation, an oasis of serenity in a desert of raging hysteria. In a mood that might have been of exaltation I had waited, awakened Cris, and then stood by while he worked on the engine.

This mood, unreal as it was, was harshly broken by the arrival of these men, particularly the officer whose gun was unholstered.

Of course I should have expected it, but I did not, and Cris's first words came with a stunning surprise, far out of proportion to their weight or meaning.

'*Bonjour, M'sieu*,' he said.

The Frenchmen said nothing. They approached us in a semicircle, hefty fellows, swarthy, unshaven as I have said, their red-rimmed eyes glittering in the light of the early sun.

Cris glanced at me.

'Do you know their language, Ned?'

'What?' I said, and then his words sank in. 'Yes, of course.'

I took a short step forward. The French captain's revolver moved a little upwards, and the whole party stopped. The suspicion was mutual, and it suddenly dawned on me that they might think we were parachutists, or that we had deliberately landed behind the lines. The red, white and blue markings on Sal made little difference.

So I said hurriedly: 'We are English.' I paused, and saw the officer's face change a little. I went on swiftly: 'We are planning to fly to England, I am a civilian and my friend has had orders to return to his English base. We have room for some passengers,' I added, and hoped that was all right with Cris.

'*M'sieu*,' said the Frenchman quietly, 'you speak excellent French, but the peculiarities of the situation are abundant, you will agree. Are you prepared to offer evidence of your *bona fides*?'

Cris stared at him curiously.

'I have my passport,' I said swiftly, 'and I have no doubt that Flying Officer St. Clare has his papers.'

'I want to get off before we're spotted from up there,' Cris said easily, and pointed skywards. 'You do the talking, Ned.'

He turned with complete detachment to one engine while I asked: 'How many can we take?'

'Ten, at a pinch. No, wait a minute.' He swung round again. 'We'd never make it with more than six, I'd forgotten this damned engine. Six, or we'll crash taking off.'

I started to explain, but was cut short.

'You will forgive my insistence, please, but your passport,' said the captain.

I did not spend time then in thinking of the absurdity of the position, but took my passport from my inside coat pocket, and handed it to him. He inspected it gravely, then returned it to me.

'*Bon, M'sieu Deane! Vous pouvez en prendre six, je comprends combien s'il y en a un d'entre eux qui doit s'etendre de tout son long.*'

'He wants to know how many if one has to lie down,' I told Cris.

'Five,' Cris said, and added: 'Ask him if he has a mechanic in his outfit.'

'*Un mecanique, mais oui, Monsieur,*' said the officer, and turned his head sharply. 'Jules, the English pilot requires assistance.' He did not wait to see the hefty *poilu* step swiftly forward, but continued to address me: 'We saw the machine before nightfall, *M'sieu*, and planned to try to get off in it at dawn. None of us knows much about aviation, it would have been a considerable risk.' He shrugged. 'We have with us our colonel, and he must be taken to England without delay, he is badly wounded.'

'But the French hospitals . . .' I began.

'Stop, please!' The man's face held an expression which really startled me, and then went on: 'Nowhere in France will be safe for the true French, *M'sieu*, take my assurance on that. Colonel Meandreux cannot walk, we shall have to carry him here. How long will it be before you can start?'

'An hour,' said Cris, without looking up. 'We'll have to try it earlier if there's an alarm, you might have your fellows keep their eyes open.'

'*Sur le champ*,' said the Frenchman, and rapped orders.

He was obeyed without question. The *poilus*, seven of them in all, began to filter through the trees, and the officer looked at me.

'Will you assist me with Colonel Meandreux?'

We tramped silently through the trees until we reached a small clearing, and, to my surprise, a little round tent, brown and green with camouflage.

A man I took to be Meandreux was stretched out on the grass. He was unconscious, and a glance at his right leg told me that his one chance of living was to have it amputated. I had spent a year as a medical student, and though I had relinquished the studies some practical knowledge of my training remained.

My companion said: 'Colonel Meandreux is a Frenchman who believes in France, and there is no room in France for such men, *M'sieu*.'

The deeper meaning of his words again escaped me; or more accurately, I paid it no attention, but said sharply:

'There'll be six feet of French soil for him unless that leg is amputated immediately.'

26

The captain looked at me searchingly, lapsing into French.

'*En Angleterre* . . .'

'We might be there in three hours, it might take twelve,' I interrupted. 'I wouldn't like to swear that the colonel will live if he keeps that for three hours.' My mind worked very swiftly then. I remembered reading that the kit of most aeroplanes included a saw, for use after a crash if the doors were blocked. 'There might be a saw in the plane,' I added. 'I am taking your word that you need to save Meandreux.'

The captain hesitated only for a moment, then said: '*Vous êtes médecin?*'

'I know enough about it for that,' I said shortly. 'Can't you see it yourself?'

'I have refused to,' he answered, then hurried out of the tent.

I looked down at the colonel's tired, strained face, then with a penknife began to cut away the clothes on the affected leg.

For the first time I had leisure to think of what the captain had said: *there was no room in France for such men*. What the deuce was he talking about? I began to find my mind filling with uncomfortable thoughts until the shadow of the captain sent them into different channels.

He carried a *poilu*'s bayonet, and Cris's saw.

There is no need to go into details of that operation. It took three-quarters of an hour, and the only thing I had to sustain me was the conviction that unless the leg was amputated within the hour it would certainly be too late to save the man's life; I was by no means sure that I was in time, even then. The task was finished at last. We made a stretcher of our coats, using the branches of two saplings as poles, and carried Meandreux to the centre of the clearing.

Cris turned from the engine, taking my end of the improvised stretcher.

He was just in time, for suddenly I went out like a light.

I felt myself falling but knew nothing else until an unfamiliar vibrating sensation roused me. When I opened my eyes I saw Cris's back in front of me, two of the *poilus* near him, Meandreux stretched out on the floor of the cabin. I retched. A man behind me pushed something over my shoulder. It was a flask. I unscrewed the cap, and the welcome fumes of whisky entered my nostrils. I took a deep, spluttering swallow.

Restored, my wits about me, I looked down through a small window.

We were flying over open country, strewn with the wreckage of war and destruction. Cris broke the long silence.

'How are you feeling, Ned?'

'I could be worse,' I said. 'So you got her up all right?'

'Scraped the trees with the wing,' Cris said, ignoring the inanity of my remark. 'We were damned nearly overloaded.' He made no further comment, and soon we were in sight of the Channel.

I must have seen it a hundred times from the French side, but never have I experienced the same feeling of exultation. We crossed the coast—made a landfall I think is the technical expression—somewhere near Hastings, but not until later did I know that we had seen the epilogue of the Dunkirk miracle.

'By the way,' I said suddenly, 'where's the captain?'

'Duval?' Cris appeared to muse. 'He's collecting one or two others, I'm going back for him.'

He said it quite casually, and the words hardly created the sensation that they should have done. His sublime certainty, to say nothing of courage, was a thing which made its full mark on me later.

It was the beginning of far greater things, too, although I did not know it then.

4

I am Brought Up-to-Date

'By the way,' said Cris as we were about to land, 'don't mention that I'm going back for Duval.' He did not turn his head, and apparently took it for granted the caution was all that was needed to ensure my silence. I know that I was prepared to accept it as a command, for I was beginning to realise exactly how much I owed to Cris.

I left everything to him. Not that I could have done anything else, of course; I mean that I was quite content to leave everything to him.

The *poilus* had said very little; I have often wondered what their thoughts must have been as we flew over the serene countryside.

An airfield loomed ahead. There were a dozen or so aircraft on the ground, the groundsmen dotted about near the runways.

Cris took us down in a perfect landing.

'The end of an adventure. Translate it for 'em, Ned.'

I did.

By the time the aerodrome staff had reached us the *poilus* were standing on English soil, and talking one against another in a high-pitched French which would have amused me but for its poignancy. I knew that they were in England for the first time in their lives, but there was something deeper in their excitement than that. It was all part of what Duval, as I now knew him to be, had told me; but not until I was talking to Sir Alan Clyde did I realise just what it was.

The station commander, a short, thickset man with a heavy black moustache, was amongst those who welcomed us. It soon transpired that several plane-loads of Frenchmen had already arrived, more often than not in their own machines, although some had come with English pilots. I heard something of Dunkirk, but it did not sink in.

Now that I was in England I had to see my chief, and every minute appeared important. I did not know exactly what was in the papers inside my coat, only that they might be of vital importance. My credentials were established, and I urged my need for getting to White-hall swiftly. The station commander put a telephone at my disposal, and soon I was talking to Clyde.

'Who?' he asked. '*Who* . . . ? Deane? Good God, I've given you up as . . . but never mind, where are you?'

'Where am I?' I asked the commander.

'Tunbridge Wells,' he said.

'Near Tunbridge Wells,' said I. 'And I've got the stuff from K.'

'Thank God for that,' said Clyde gravely. 'Get a car . . . No, let me have a word with the C.O., that'll be quicker.'

It was not often that Clyde gave any hint of excitement, and I found it contagious. The C.O. took the instrument, and Cris eyed me with the smile which I had grown to know well.

'You're a dark horse, Ned,' he said. 'I didn't know you were a Whitehall wallah. Just in case we lose touch, what's your address?'

'When I'm in London, 88b Clarges Street,' I said. 'But you'll be as likely to find me at the Whitehall Club.'

'R.A.F. Club, me,' said Cris. 'Or St. Clare House, near Dorchester. Look me up when and if you can, won't you?' He spoke as if he was genuinely anxious not to lose touch with me. 'Good luck, Ned. I didn't need the compass, but I won't forget those cigarettes for a long time.'

'I won't forget . . .' I began, but the C.O., now finished with Clyde, broke in with:

'I'll have some sandwiches prepared for you, Mr. Deane, and there'll be a car at your disposal in a quarter of an hour. If you'd like a wash . . .' He paused, and I said quickly that I would very much like one. 'Look after Mr. Deane, St. Clare, will you?' said the C.O.

'Yes, sir,' said Cris.

We did not talk a great deal in the cloakroom. After a quick wash Cris took me to the car, then waiting outside with a W.A.A.F. girl at the wheel. I turned and looked at Cris.

'Happy landings,' I said.

We shook hands; it was the first time. I climbed in, choosing the back seat, and the girl drove off smartly. I looked through the rear window and saw Cris standing and staring after me. He waved as we turned out of the gates of the aerodrome.

I drew out my last cigarette, my mind in a whirl of emotions. That finished, I turned to the W.A.A.F. driver.

'Do you happen to have a cigarette?' I asked a little

awkwardly. 'Or if you could pull up near a shop, I could get some.'

She said she had a case which was nearly full, and slowed down to get it from her pocket. Then I decided to sit in the front with her; I was hungry for word of what had been happening in England.

'I think I'll come up in front,' I said, and she pulled into the side of road, making no comment.

I asked a tentative question; what did she think of the general situation?

'Think of it?' She shot me a sideways glance, and laughed shortly. 'It hardly bears thinking about, does it?' Startled, I told her that I had not been in England for three months, and had not looked at an English paper or heard an English broadcast for more than a month.

What she told me electrified me.

Chamberlain out, Churchill in. Dunkirk. Pétain and his military dictatorship. Daladier and Reynaud thrown to the wolves, the Nazis near Paris, rumours that it was to be declared an open city. The collapse of France a probability. Italy in the war. Gradually my mind began to protest at the burden imposed on it; there were too many shocks to take in and understand in so short a time.

I groped for another cigarette, and lit it blindly. Then the things began to take on a different perspective, and one stood out above all others.

Churchill in, Chamberlain out.

'Thank God for that,' I said.

'What?' asked my driver.

'The new Prime Minister,' I said.

'He's . . .' She hesitated, and then said simply: 'He's grand. God knows what would have happened had Chamberlain been leading us now. It's so like England to see sense only at the eleventh hour. This time, though, it may be too late.' She spoke with the sober wisdom of a mature woman, but I knew she could not know just what invasion would mean.

We had now turned into Trafalgar Square, and were going along Whitehall. I told her exactly where to stop, and then asked:

'What were your instructions?'

'To return as soon as you were here, sir.'

I felt sorry. I am not a susceptible man, but she was the first normal-looking woman or girl I had seen for a long time. Her outlook was direct and refreshing, her poise and courage fine. She might be scared but she would face whatever was to come without hesitation.

She left the car while I was climbing out, and saluted.

'Damn that,' I said, and shook hands. She looked at me, her eyes direct and grey; I think she was smiling a little. I plunged my free hand into my pocket and drew out my empty cigarette case; it was a gold one, finely monogrammed, a twenty-first birthday present from my father.

'A souvenir,' I said hurriedly. 'A memento, call it what you like. Thanks. Goodbye.' I thrust it into her hand and turned hastily away, without looking over my shoulder, as I entered the door of the Whitehall building where I knew I would find Sir Alan Clyde.

I cannot try to pretend to understand the emotions which filled me, the sentiment which possessed me. I have never seen that girl again, but I shall never forget her.

From the shadows of the hall a man in khaki approached me, his bayonet fixed.

'I want to see Sir Alan Clyde,' I said testily. 'He knows I'm coming, I'll go straight up.'

'You'll need a permit for that, sir.' There was a tinge

of respect in the man's words, although there had been none in his first peremptory challenge.

From the corridor came a hurrying figure, the middle-aged, trim little woman I knew as Clyde's secretary.

'Mr. Deane,' she began, and then broke off abruptly. I had never seen Jane Nicholson taken aback before.

'What the deuce is the matter?' I demanded. 'Anyone would think you'd seen a ghost.'

'N-no,' said Jane. 'Not a ghost, Mr. Deane.' She swallowed again, and spoke a word of reassurance to the sentry. Then she walked with me to the lift. I was only dimly beginning to comprehend what a wreck I looked when she opened the door of Clyde's office.

He was not alone; I recognised Henby, the Foreign Under-Secretary, and Myall, an attaché to the Berlin Embassy before the opening of hostilities. All of them looked towards me, and all gaped.

Clyde recovered first as he stepped forward with outstretched hand.

'My dear chap, you look all in.' His hand gripped mine. 'You . . .' He stopped. I have a reputation for sartorial meticulousness, and I realised, then, in an overwhelming wave, what kind of impression I had created.

The change in my make-up since the days when I had rebelled against the F.O. appointment had been deeper perhaps than I knew. I had become pedantic, precise, even dapper; watching Clyde's face and that of the others, I saw myself as they had seen me then. The contrast to now must have hit them quite a bit. Sketchily washed, unshaven, shabby, I had not given it a thought, and what was more, I did not care what I looked like. My smile was tinged with grimness as I said:

'I have the papers, sir.' I took off my coat, exposing a torn and soiled shirt unchanged for three weeks. I was

34

inwardly amused at the shocked expression on Henby's face. I could imagine the effort it took him not to wrinkle his nose. 'Can you lend me a knife?'

'A—knife?' echoed Clyde faintly. He handed me a penknife and I ripped the lining of my coat and extracted the papers.

'I haven't examined them,' I said formally. 'I don't know . . .' I stopped, and my head nodded. 'Not to my credit that they're here, a Flying Officer . . .'

I went to sleep.

Looking back I realise that I have not made so good a job as I might have done in describing my return to England. There's little I can do about it, because my memory is vague about many of my impressions and feelings. Apart from that, there was my fatigue; I don't think that anything really registered once the parcel was in Clyde's hand.

I only vaguely remember being moved from the office, and hearing voices, the jolting of a car, the opening of doors, hands about my body pulling at my clothes. I wished they would leave me alone.

Eventually I slept, heavily.

It was not an untroubled sleep. The chief recollections I have of its dreams are of my first meeting with Cris, the blowing-up of the cottage, the moment when I saw the Frenchman, Duval; and, finally, and by far the most vivid, the chicken. I had a dream about that chicken almost from its pullet stage. It was with me all the time, even in Clyde's office. I remembered the dream, and others which followed, for weeks on end. I cannot eat chicken to this day without a shudder.

I was vague and uncertain in my mind, although I remember waking up in a sweat of fear, and hearing a soothing voice speak to me. Something warm was put into my mouth, and a spoon grated against my teeth. I only know that when at last I did wake up, not refreshed but no longer so tired, with a heavy headache and a brackish taste in my mouth, I was in a handsomely furnished bedroom. A middle-aged nurse was sitting by a window, knitting.

'Hallo,' I croaked.

The nurse put down her knitting at once. She approached me hurriedly.

'That's more like it,' she said. 'Don't try to sit up, I'll help you.'

She did so, with quiet efficiency. My body was aching as if it were bruised all over, but I was sitting comfortably at last, and my mind was clear. Because of that I did not rush into a lot of questions, but allowed things to take their own course.

Some time later an oldish doctor came in to take a look at me.

'You'll do,' he said. 'Stay in bed for the rest of the day, and you'll be able to get up in the morning.'

'I'd like to see Sir Alan Clyde,' I said, as firmly as my voice would allow.

'That shouldn't be difficult,' answered the doctor. 'You're in his house.'

I could not have been awake more than two hours before I was fast asleep again. This time I did not dream, and felt really refreshed when I awakened.

I learned that I had been in bed for five days, and found, when I attempted to stand, that my legs would not carry me. By the evening, however, I was able to walk fairly easily round the room.

Clyde had sent to my flat for some clothes, and when I went down to dinner I was smoothly shaven and well dressed for the first time for a month.

'Hallo, Ned,' said Clyde as I entered the dining-room. He was alone, and the table was set for two.

'Hallo,' said I. 'I was wondering—here, what the hell are you talking about? Ned?'

Clyde chuckled. 'I've seen St. Clare,' he told me.

'Have you, indeed. How is he?'

'Nursing a sprained ankle,' said Clyde. 'What did you think of him?'

'I can't find the necessary words,' I told him, 'and it's no use trying. He—no, it's no use.' I forked some *hors-d'œuvres*, then looked sharply into Clyde's face. 'He *is* all right?'

'I should say he has been thoroughly enjoying himself,' Clyde assured me. 'He's been back to that spot where you came from, and pulled in nearly thirty more French officers. Duval arranged to get them there.'

'Good Lord! So he did go back.'

'He went back off his own bat,' said Clyde, 'and then persuaded the authorities that he could bring a lot of useful men out of France. He has done, and others are doing so too. We need all we can get.'

'Yes,' I said. 'Oh, how's the colonel?'

'Meandreux? Well enough to want to say "Thanks".'

'Poor chap, it's a miracle he survived.'

We talked rather idly over dinner. Clyde did nothing to lead the conversation in any particular channel, and I gave him a fairly comprehensive story of what had happened to me. As I talked, a burning rage welled up when I remembered the refugees, the insensate bombing, the machine-gunning, the use of the civil population as a cover for advancing troops. That burning sensation, almost choking me, faded after a while, but it has never completely disappeared.

Clyde listened with few interruptions.

He is a big man, on the portly side, grey-haired, imposing-looking rather than handsome. His smile, like Cris's, is infectious. I knew he had stormed against Whitehall's mishandling of the Nazi menace for years, and had been in considerable trouble with the Cabinet from time to time; nevertheless he remained the F.O.'s political adviser. He knew more about Germany, I think, than any man living.

Finally I ran dry.

Clyde pulled at his underlip.

'Not the best of times to live through, Ned.'

'No,' I said.

'We owe you a lot,' Clyde went on thoughtfully. 'Those papers . . .' He paused.

'Yes?' I said eagerly.

'They contain a fairly comprehensive list of the French officers who are reliable,' said Clyde. 'The men we want for the Free French Force, of course.' I had read the papers, and knew something about de Gaulle. 'The Boche wanted the list badly, and knew K. had it. You reached him just in time. Yes, we're grateful, although you probably won't think so in a few minutes. After you've had a rest we've a new job for you. But not,' he added quietly, 'in the Foreign Office.'

5

I Meet Relatives of Cris

I experienced a faint sensation of shock at his words, but nothing like the sensation which I think he had expected. Had I given any thought to it, I suppose I might have expected to be told of promotion, of an appointment somewhere abroad with rather more responsibility than I had yet been given. Granted that expectancy, my disappointment would have been acute.

'No?' I said mildly.

Clyde chuckled.

'That's better than I expected, anyhow. The idea was mine, and . . .'

I said abruptly: 'France?'

Clyde's hazel eyes narrowed, and he seemed to be looking at a place just beneath my chin.

'No, not that, Ned. Something less heroic, if heroic's the word, and safer, too. We can't use your experience and abilities in Europe; there isn't any room. We're doing no more than keeping the Embassies open, and taking reports. Except in Greece and Yugoslavia, they're all under German control.' He was quite sure of himself, and I realised that it was wholly true; it was not a pleasant admission, for when last I had been in England, Holland, Belgium and France had appeared to be ramparts, insecure as far as the first two were concerned, but nevertheless substantial as a unit. I had not yet realised the full implications of the fact that the French Army was no longer a factor of importance on our side.

'There's just one way of getting information to the occupied countries,' Clyde went on. 'That's by radio. With your knowledge of languages . . .'

He stopped, and I stared at him.

I had not been in Germany so long without listening to a lot of our foreign language broadcasts. They had not been impressive, and I had often been restless because of the lack of imagination shown in the approach to the German people. I knew their mood. They would listen to only one voice apart from Hitler's—that of fear. They had to be insidiously poisoned with the fear of vengeance. One day, given that, the poison would affect them all.

'What I've suggested,' Clyde went on at last, 'is that you go over to the B.B.C. As a broadcaster,' he added. 'We've a new liaison officer, and there's a different system going into operation. You know a lot of the people, you know the countries, and you can help a great deal as well as do the reading. It's on the vague side, as yet, but I want your reaction to it.'

I eyed him steadily.

Few men have a greater claim to my respect or my liking. I have dined in his house frequently, and might call myself a friend of the family, but there has always been a suspicion of unapproachability about him. Perhaps it would be fairer and more accurate to say that he had never appeared to take me wholly into his confidence; I have had an impression that despite his apparent trust I have always been on trial. That is understandable enough. Few men have been so frequently betrayed by subordinates who have incautiously expressed private opinions of their own, widely at variance with his official ones.

I thought then that there was appeal in Clyde's eyes. Perhaps it was imagination. Certainly I had no idea at the time of the real motive behind his suggestion, the many things he and others were planning.

'Look here,' I said, 'you don't want me to pump drivel over the air, do you?'

Clyde drew a deep breath.

'No, not that. I'll tell you what you will have to do.' He pushed his chair back. 'We'll go next door for some coffee, and we won't be disturbed.'

What followed is no longer confidential.

There have been several books written on the subject, some of them shrewd guesses by their authors who have been astonishingly close to the mark. I do not propose to go into details, for my long period with the B.B.C. was not particularly exciting or interesting, except for a brief period I shall mention. But I sat and listened to Clyde's exposition of what was little more, then, than an idea, with breathless interest.

The need for talking to a France under the German heel was a completely new eventuality, for I don't think any official mind had ever accepted the possibility of the downfall of France until it was upon us, and the country was told: *'We will fight on the beaches and in the fields . . . if necessary alone.'* That 'alone' was the operative word which awakened the country to the true situation as nothing else had done.

Clyde now put before me a plan for talking in the first place to the people of France, while at the same time communicating by code to certain individuals there. The messages would be heard by the Nazi radio-ears, but the code would be secret and understood only by the few for whom it was intended.

Here, as I saw it, was a potential weapon beyond words to describe. The strong but temporarily impotent anti-Axis elements could be co-ordinated and kept in touch with London just as London kept in touch with others in the earlier occupied zones.

We had coffee, and liqueurs, as Clyde elaborated this plan. A clock struck one o'clock, then two. Not until some time after that did he finish, and run a hand through his mane of grey hair.

'Well, Ned, what do you think of it?'

'I'm in,' I said without hesitating. 'I don't need a rest . . .'

'You're going to have one,' Clyde said firmly. 'St. Clare is on sick leave, nursing that sprained ankle. He wants you to go to Dorchester for a week. It's a pity in some ways that he's in the R.A.F. But he'll be kept busy enough when they have their shot at us.'

'Do you think they will really attempt an invasion?' I asked.

'Only God, the Navy and the R.A.F. can stop them,' said Clyde soberly. 'And before that they might do a lot of damage. Not that it affects our plans,' he added. He was the most confident man I know, and I realised that he was feeling something of the exaltation which I had felt when I had been hemmed in by the trees near Crève-cœur.

For some reason we shook hands before going to bed.

I went to my flat for the first time the next morning, packed enough for seven days at St. Clare House, and caught the half past one train from Waterloo. I was excited at the thought of seeing Cris, as well as at the prospects of the new job. My one regret was that I could not discuss it with him.

He was waiting for me at Dorchester Station.

Looking back, I can remember the car, and the girl sitting at the wheel. It is a queer fact that I cannot recall, in any exactitude, my first impression of her. I only saw her then as a part of the *ensemble*, of which the centre-piece was Cris. I carried my case to the car, dropped it, and gripped Cris's hands.

He grinned widely.

'My, my, they've been feeding you up, I wouldn't have recognised you! Sheila, this is the Ned you've been so curious about.' He beamed happily. 'My sister,' he added. 'Anything that has come out of France for the last month is an object of her insatiable curiosity, and she'll want to know all about everything.'

'Brotherly revenge,' explained Sheila lightly. 'He wanted to drive, and I wouldn't let him.'

She was wearing no hat, and her hair was blowing becomingly in the wind.

'You'd better get in,' she said practically.

I rounded the car with her, deposited the luggage on the empty seat after she had climbed in, and then joined Cris. He said little, and after a while I mentioned that I had heard he had been back to France.

He shrugged. 'So you know that? They don't know at home, and I don't want them to. Only Sheila.'

'Right,' I said. 'Is Duval still in France?'

'He should be on the way here by now,' Cris said soberly. 'He was to make the final trip early this morning. With any luck, he'll be with us tonight.'

'With us!' I exclaimed involuntarily.

Cris smiled. 'Why not? He's nowhere else to go until the Free French get into some kind of order, and I thought he might as well make up the party. I've grown quite attached to Anton,' he added, his smile widening. 'We even swear at each other in French.' More soberly: 'If there were six million like him, this débâcle would never have happened.'

Sheila turned the Rolls-Royce off the main road

through an imposing gateway bearing the crest of a lion and a dove on each pillar. There was a long drive ahead of us lined with beech. Those trees gave me my first impression of the age of St. Clare House.

There was a spaciousness about the grounds which impressed me, but nothing like as much as the house. House? I have rarely seen anything closer approaching a castle which had not been dubbed one! A moat surrounded it, and although the drawbridge had gone and a permanent structure built in its place, the original chains of the bridge were still there.

Inside, St. Clare House was as distinctive as the grounds. Say what you like about the 'stately homes of England', for sheer historic atmosphere, there is nothing to approach them.

I grew familiar over a period with the whole set-up, although it was only that night that I realised Cris's family was one of the oldest and most honourable in England. The name was familiar enough, once I allowed myself to think about it.

His mother was away, but I met his father for the first time that evening. An older man than I had expected, he was, I could see, much loved by his son and daughter.

Some time after ten o'clock Jameson, the butler, came with a card. He took it to Cris, who glanced down and then laughed aloud.

'Duval's got a nice touch, Ned.'

'Is he here?' I asked quickly.

'Yes,' said Cris. 'I'll come, Jameson.' He went out, and the rest of us sat without talking.

I find it difficult to explain what happened then, unless I use the plain old-fashioned word jealousy. That is surely absurd, for I could not have been in love with Sheila at that time. Or could I? At all events, I felt

44

vaguely that I had left the centre of the stage, and that Duval was going to take it from me. I remembered him as good-looking, and could imagine him making a deep impression on women.

I remember that Sheila's eyes were glistening, and she was looking towards the door. No more than that, and once she glanced at me, but I doubt whether she saw me.

Voices outside, and then Duval entered.

I don't know to this day where he obtained his spotless uniform, but it was there, with the Cross of the Legion d'Honneur fastened to the breast of the jacket. He looked bigger than I remembered, and certainly far better-looking.

Sheila stood up swiftly; I noticed that.

Duval bowed over her hand; I remember wondering if he were going to kiss it, but he spared me that. He bowed to St. Clare, assuring him that he had taken dinner on the way down, accepted an easy chair and, with his excellent but accented English, began then and there to take the limelight.

After an hour of resentful silence I realised that I was making an ass of myself, and stirred myself to greater efforts. I don't think anyone noticed the period of my sulkiness, and by the next morning I was ashamed of it. That may have been, of course, when I found that Sheila was completely impartial; at the time I don't think she considered either of us as anything but rather exciting, probably giving us far more glamour, if that is the right word, than either of us deserved. I was down to breakfast early, and was rewarded with twenty minutes of Sheila on my own. Then Cris arrived, and a little later Duval came in.

'No, no, Sheila,' he said quickly, 'don't get up, please, I can help myself.' He went to the sideboard and selected

45

sausages and eggs, while I contemplated in silent admiration the man who could call Sheila by her Christian name with such ease and on so short an acquaintance.

Lady St. Clare returned in the middle of the week, full of the idea, which she proposed to carry out at once, of turning the house into a convalescent home. She brought with her three slightly wounded pilots, who helped to make the party merry, and on the Saturday there was a cricket match in which Duval again distinguished himself.

For all of us at St. Clare House it was a time of rest and recuperation, but before the full week was up I grew restless to know more about the B.B.C. proposition. I phoned Clyde, who sent me down some books on the technical side of broadcasting. The next day some notes on the formation of the new enterprise reached me, and I found myself making suggestions and advising alterations; I was deep in the work, and for two days spent little time out of the big room they had allotted to me. If any of them were curious they said nothing.

Cris had left on Sunday evening to report to his squadron. Duval was to see the Free French leaders on the following day, while I was summoned to appear at Broadcasting House.

We were known as *Foreign Service, F2*. We had a room of our own, a staff of linguists and another staff of political experts, all carefully chosen. Gradually we evolved a code and a system, and on the 1st of July I went to the microphone for the first time. In addition to F2, of course, there were other departments broadcasting to France, but ours was the only one that passed messages in code.

I was perspiring freely when I went to the microphone. I had no idea how many Frenchmen and women were going to listen, nor did I know that in parts of the

46

occupied zone it was already tantamount to a death sentence to be discovered listening-in to England.

I became the Voice that night, calling to the people of France to rally to the old cry of *Liberté, egalité, fraternité*. I told them how they had been tricked and cheated, and I named the worst of the quislings then known to us.

It caused, we learnt afterwards, a minor sensation.

Soon reports filtered in of the murder of some of those named. France was rising, the paralysis of disaster was beginning to fade. More and more Frenchmen escaped from the Channel coast, or came through Spain, rallying to the cause.

In France, I learned, I became the Voice, but I don't recall being particularly proud of myself. Heaven knows I had no cause to be, for I was but a mouthpiece. Nevertheless, I was immersed in the job. I more than liked it; I loved it.

When eventually the studio moved out of London and settled in the West Country I was sorry. However, to the West Country I was sent, and I found that I was within forty miles of Dorchester. Consequently when Cris telephoned me one day and suggested I spent another weekend there, I agreed not only with alacrity but the knowledge that I was reasonably near 'home' in any emergency.

I spent several weekends at St. Clare House, enjoying them, growing more aware of Sheila's importance to me. The fifth weekend was to be in early January, and I was looking forward to it with more than usual zest, for Cris as well as Sheila were to be there and there was a chance that Duval would also be with us.

It was during that fifth weekend at St. Clare that they first tried to kill me.

6

I am Lucky to Escape

The Sunday was bitterly cold, but fine and clear. The papers had arrived early from London, and the household breathed with relief; we took the time of their arrival from London as an indication of the severity of the previous night's raid. Practically the whole of life was coloured by the attack on London, and even being used to the fact was no protection against the depression it caused. To offset the depression there was, at times, a brittle and unreal gaiety, a determined, deliberate cheerfulness without foundation.

Lady St. Clare had arranged a London office for her convalescent home, and Sheila was often there; both of them staying overnight in London when the need arose, refusing to let high explosives or incendiaries drive them away. I admired their spirit but wished Sheila could be somewhere else.

Some twenty-five R.A.F. men were at St. Clare that weekend, most of them well enough to walk about. The lake had frozen over, and on the Saturday evening there had been a great hunt through the house for skates.

The Saturday's general if irreverent prayer was that the ice would hold next day. Sheila was looking forward to it, but I am no great performer and would have viewed with more than equanimity the prospect of a sudden thaw.

This proved, however, to be a vain hope.

Duval had arrived, and had been on the ice before breakfast; it was superb, he said. Sheila, who had been with him, agreed. Cris had turned in late the night before, and was not up when most of us went to the lake; he called out, however, that he would view the fun from his bedroom window.

'Loafer!' called Sheila. 'Ned will start you in figure 8's.'

'I don't believe he can do a half-turn,' Cris retorted, and my heart sank. If I succeeded it would be by good fortune more than anything else. I found myself next to Sheila with Duval on the other side.

'Seriously,' I muttered nervously, 'I'm no use at all. Isn't there a small, shallow pond where I can potter about at my leisure, instead of taking up the room more properly used by the experts?'

Duval laughed; he had a pleasant laugh, that of a man who enjoyed his life and his jokes alike.

He shot a wicked glance at me, knowing full well that I did not want to make a fool of myself, for I had confessed my apprehension to him the night before.

Sheila decided to take me seriously.

'There is a little pond at the end of the lake, if you're really a beginner, Ned. Anton can come and give you a lesson or two. If he can keep going long enough,' she added, and Duval laughed again. He had told me that he frequently entered the French Indoor Skating Championship events.

In the distance I could see that one or two beginners were already using the small pond, and I felt cheered when I recognised one of them as Nobby Baynes, who had shot down twenty-three German machines to the public knowledge, and as many more if his squadron was to be believed. Sheila supervised the fastening of my skates, and watched while I went gingerly on to the ice. By some miracle I avoided collapsing, and made a more or less successful trip to the other side and back. I noticed half-way across that a barrel was on the ice near one edge, with a board nailed on, reading 'DANGEROUS PAST HERE'. If I kept about thirty yards from it, I thought, I would be safe enough. Duval was executing some fancy steps near Sheila before she joined him and they went off together, towards the lake. After a few minutes Nobby Baynes and his companions went off too, deciding to watch the fun of the experts performing. I was alone then, wondering if it were worth it, yet fascinated by the task of keeping my balance. I think a faint jealousy of Duval was one of the reasons; he always had the ability to stir me a little, although by then I not only liked him but regarded him as a friend.

I was going steadily across the pond when I heard a crack. I jerked my head round, and as I did so something passed my face like an angry bee.

Down I went.

There was another crack, and this time I saw a bullet kick up a little flurry of ice near my feet.

It sobered me. I could hear the echo of the shot in my mind, and I knew it had come from the left, where there was a roadway running through the estate. I looked towards it, not fully realising that I was being shot at, but knowing enough to be scared.

I saw the flash of the third shot as it nicked the shoulder of my coat.

At that I grew nearer to panic than I had been since Cris had introduced himself at the cottage, but for the life of me I could not get up. I tried and slipped, tried again and fell heavily.

After another futile attempt I began to propel myself across the ice with my hands. I heard shouting, and fancied that my name was called, but I did not look round. The ice was slippery, and my steering clumsy. Before I knew where I was I had passed the barrel, and heard the ice crack beneath me. The crack suddenly widened, and down I went head first into the water. I struck out wildly, but only for a moment. Then reason came to my rescue and I behaved more sanely. I remained desperately frightened, but my head and shoulder broke water and I took in a deep breath of air.

Figures were moving on the bank, and something fell close by me. It was the end of a rope. I made a grab, and caught it. By then I was so cold that my teeth were chattering, and the pain in my legs and thighs was almost unbearable.

Slowly I was dragged to safety. Two or three of the R.A.F. men helped me up the bank, while someone called out:

'Run him to the house, he'll be all right.'

My arms were seized and willy-nilly I was hustled towards the house. I doubt whether any of them suspected the shooting; there was no hint of it. Halfway to the house I saw Cris, dashing from the porch.

'You all right?' His voice was hardly recognisable.

'Y-y-yes,' I stammered.

'Upstairs and into a hot bath!' he cried out as he went past me. Stormed past me is probably the better way of describing his progress and had I been less cold and miserable I might have attempted to stop him. But my companions gave me little time to pause as they hustled me upstairs to a bathroom.

Sinking into near-boiling water did wonders, thawing both body and mind. After a brisk rub down and a hot toddy in my room, my mind began a series of violent acrobatics.

51

I decided that I had been shot at; possibly by accident, possibly not. And if not, why?

I found this question unanswerable, and I was about to rise wearily to get into some clothes when there was a tap on the door. Jameson entered.

He is a family servant whom one takes for granted at a house like St. Clare; the soul of discretion, and enemy of all things sensational. I do not know whether he approved of the convalescent home idea, but am sure he disapproved of some of the brighter spirits amongst the guests.

'I hope you're feeling better, sir,' he said.

'Much better, Jameson, thanks. It was a crazy thing to do, wasn't it?'

'I wasn't at the spot, sir,' said Jameson neatly, and turned to someone I could not see. 'I'll take those, Nellie, thank you.' He reappeared with a tray on which were the various oddments which I knew had been taken from my pockets, and my coat.

'I thought you would like these, sir,' said Jameson, 'and that you ought to see this.' He held the coat gingerly by the collar, bringing it to me with the right shoulder foremost.

The tear in it was unmistakable.

My heart sank as I regarded it.

'Yes, Jameson, thanks,' I said. 'Leave it, will you?'

He bowed, and went out. I went across to a table and helped myself to another whisky, this time considerably stronger. It was not pleasant to think that death had come so near, and even less so to admit that there had been an attempt, deliberate and cold-blooded, to kill me.

'This won't do,' I said aloud, and jumped to my feet.

I had on everything but shoes and coat when there was

a bang rather than a tap on the door, and before I had finished saying 'Come in' the door burst open and Cris entered.

There are times when he is just a young man with a smile and a way with him, and others when he is something much more than that. I suppose it is some kind of personal magnetism. Many people have it in a greater or lesser degree, but in the case of public figures it is usually created as much by the audience as by the man. Moreover the audience probably inspires the man; it is a mutual quality, and in many cases the man without his audience would be quite ordinary. In the very few the audience does not really take any part. The power, spirit, influence, call it what you will, emanates from the man and needs no mirror to give a reflection and increase its brilliance.

Cris is such a man. I think that was the first time I fully realised it.

'Well, Ned,' he said. 'This is a pretty kettle of fish. You weren't hurt?'

'No,' I said, 'they didn't do much damage, but they got precious near it.' I picked up the coat and handed it to him.

'Not bad shooting,' he said. 'I heard the shots from the window, but didn't get more than a glimpse of the sharpshooter. Anton and Sheila missed him, as they had to stop to take off their skates. Not that they could have done much. Anton didn't have a gun with him.'

I swallowed hard.

'So—they know?'

'Oh yes. They were nearer you than any of the others, and realised at once that the sound was a shot and not the cracking of the ice.' He looked at me steadily.

'Why the devil should anyone shoot at me?' I demanded

53

helplessly. 'Was it a mistake? Were they after someone else?'

'Good Lord, no.'

'But why shoot at me? Why . . . ?'

'Don't be that dumb-witted, Ned,' implored Cris. 'They've a sound enough reason. The Voice is one of the most potent weapons being used against Hitler, you must know that. What I can't understand is how the devil they knew *you* were the Voice?'

I stared at him.

Although he had answered the first questions, I knew he was speaking as much to himself as to me, but that realisation faded in another, newer, stranger one.

I accepted the presumption that if I had been deliberately attacked it was because of the Voice. It bears repeating that the context of my broadcasts was the thing that mattered, not the man who read them, yet the personal touch which it is possible to put over the ether does have an effect; judge your own reaction, critical and often unfavourable, of new B.B.C. announcers the first two or three times they are on the air. It was not difficult to understand that the Nazis would consider it worth trying to force a change. I suppose that from the first I had really understood the reason, but shied from it. I did not know then that the issue was to go far wider than the attempt on my life, that I was no more than a cypher in the game.

I doubt whether I thought of that then, and if I did, the ideas flashed past one another swiftly, leaving me with one question which I was almost too stupefied to ask. But I contrived to keep my voice even as I said:

'Nor can I, Cris. But how did *you* know that I was the Voice?' For the life of me I could not repress the emphasis on the 'you' as I stared into his face.

7

Conclave of Five

Cris continued to look through me rather than at me, and I repeated the question.

'Sorry, Ned,' he said. 'I wasn't listening.'

'I've repeated it twice,' I complained with a touch of irritation. 'How did you know?'

He shrugged.

'I've known for some time, old man. No, you haven't let it out, you've maintained the secret well enough. I've often felt like congratulating you.' He relaxed and sat on the arm of my chair. 'Clyde told me some time back,' he added briefly. 'Things are often not what they seem, you know.' He made that cryptic utterance casually, and went on in a stronger, sharper voice: 'We get back to the main questions: how did your assailant know you were the Voice, and how was it that he was in a position to attack you?'

I flicked the ash from my cigarette.

'One way and the other it's getting beyond me,' I admitted. 'As far as I can see, killing me wouldn't be of much purpose; Clyde could quite easily get someone else to take over.'

'Yes, but time would be lost before your successor could gain the confidence of his listeners,' went on Cris, 'if he ever did. I've listened to you half a dozen times, and you put something into it which a lot of people just haven't got. It's more than feeling, far more than histrionics on a leash. You're the voice of England. I doubt whether you could do it but for that fortnight you had last year, and I'm sure you don't realise it's there. However, this won't make any progress, and we've got to make some. Sheila and Anton will be in soon. They know that you were shot at, but Sheila doesn't know you're the Voice.'

'And Anton?' I was even more startled.

'Yes,' said Cris briefly. 'And he also knows why it isn't wise to report this attack yet. Until you've told Clyde, at all events. Sheila won't, and I fancy she'll be demanding the police. Can you keep her quiet? Put up some story about doing work in high places without specifying what it is?' He eyed me keenly.

'Yes,' I said. 'But I'm not sure the police oughtn't to be told now. They needn't know everything.' I was really grappling with the statement that Anton Duval knew of my identity, that closely guarded secret as I had thought.

'They can't do much,' Cris said. 'The trail's cold already. Of course, if you really make a point of it . . .' He paused.

'I'll phone Clyde,' I promised.

'I'll do that,' said Cris. 'You concentrate on Sheila.'

I had not heard footsteps outside until he finished speaking. Then they were unmistakable.

There was a brief interlude on the threshold before Sheila and Anton entered.

'We missed him!' Sheila cried tragically. 'We were as slow as snails. Why oh why didn't we move faster! Have you told the police?'

Duval was looking at me intently.

'No,' I said. 'And I'm not going to, yet at all events.'

'But that's absurd,' protested Sheila. 'The beast *shot* at you, I *saw* him. You did too, Anton.' Duval nodded, as she turned the full force of her persuasive armament on me. 'I'm not going to let you do nothing, Ned. The devil deserves hanging.'

'Not at the moment,' I said hastily, spreading my hands towards the fire. 'I don't want to go to the police until I've had a chance of talking to my chief.'

'What's your chief got to do with it?' demanded Sheila scathingly. '*You* were shot at.'

'*Chérie* . . .' began Anton.

'This is between Ned and me,' said Sheila firmly. 'You've been trying to talk me out of going to the police all the way back, and I'm not listening. Ned, you *must* see sense. If you don't call them quickly the—the trail will be dead.'

'If it isn't dead already,' I said, remembering Cris's comment. I smiled at her again, and proffered cigarettes. 'Actually I'm not so sure it's anything to get worked up about,' I went on.

That unleashed the storm.

I might not think my life worth anything, said Sheila, but others did. In any case, was I of the opinion that they wanted a friend murdered, and the inevitable investigation and inconvenience? I looked at her quickly, for an idea sprang into my mind for the first time: that she was worried and concerned because of the personal factor. It had a warming effect on me, and served the temporary purpose of driving all other thoughts out of my mind.

Anton, aware, I suppose, of the dangers of over-persuasion, stood with his back to the window, grave-faced but, I thought, inwardly amused. I retorted to Sheila in kind, and a stranger who knew no better might have thought that we were quarrelling.

Finally she shrugged her shoulders, and said: 'All right, if you really feel like that. But tell me one thing. Had you any idea that it might happen?'

'Not the foggiest,' I said earnestly. 'I would certainly have arranged it somewhere else if I had.'

'Idiot,' said Sheila. 'I'm not sure that you're fit to be left alone.' She tossed the half-smoked cigarette into the fire, and shook out her curls. 'I'm beginning to think,' she went on slowly, 'that you're a dark horse, Ned. I remember how secretive you were the first week you were here, skulking in your room for most of two days. Remember, Anton?'

'Vaguely,' murmured Anton. 'Am I admitted to the party again, *Mam'selle*?' He bowed ironically.

'You're as bad as Ned,' Sheila told him, adding shrewdly: 'I wouldn't be surprised if you knew something about it, too.' She half-turned towards the door, and then looked back at me. Already I was realising that she had noticed how I had kept to my room during the first week, and my cheeks were a little flushed. 'Ned,' she said. 'Be careful, won't you?'

Then she went out.

Anton coughed gently.

'So that is how it is, Ned? On this point, then, we are enemies, for it is like that with me too.'

I stared at Anton, momentarily bewildered.

I know the French fairly well, but their astonishing frankness in matters of the heart never ceases to come as a surprise.

For some seconds I did not fully realise what he meant, and then I coloured, drawing a deep breath.

'Damn it, Anton . . .'

'I wish,' he went on, 'that I had your chance, for already it seems to me that she is half in love with you.'

I swallowed hard.

Before he could say more, Cris was back in the room, and never have I been so thankful to see him.

'Clyde's on the way here, Ned,' he said abruptly, 'and wants you to hold everything until he's arrived.'

'A man of action!' exclaimed Anton calmly. 'There is something about Clyde I like very much.'

'How the devil do *you* know him?' I ejaculated.

Anton smiled and spread his hands.

'I too have my secrets,' he said. 'Be patient, Ned, and after lunch you will know everything, or nearly everything.'

Cris turned to me.

'Ned, you've another job to do. Show yourself in the grounds, and tell everyone what a fool you were for venturing so close to the danger spot. No one saw the shooting except we three.'

'Someone else knows about it,' I said.

'Who?' asked Cris swiftly.

'Jameson,' said I.

'Jameson?'

'Ned, you imbecile!' exclaimed Anton. 'Surely you have not talked to Jameson!' He turned and eyed Cris in desolation. 'We should not leave him alone, Sheila was right.'

'Don't be an ass,' I said irritably. 'Jameson took my clothes, and there was a bullet score across the coat shoulder. He brought it to my notice. I said nothing, but the man's not a fool.'

Anton grimaced, and Cris said:

'I think I'd better have a word with Jameson. He isn't likely to talk, but it's as well to be on the safe side.'

I put on a coat and scarf, and left the room after Cris, in company with Anton. Halfway along the passage to the stairs he stopped abruptly and faced me with a tragic expression on his face.

'Ned!'

'What the devil's the matter now?' He really alarmed me.

'You have forgotten your skates.'

I drew a deep breath, but was chuckling when we reached the hall.

A log fire was burning in the enormous fireplace, and half a dozen of the R.A.F. men were gathered about it. They called out their solicitations, and I waved a reply before going into the cold air.

It was getting near to lunchtime, and there were few skaters, but those there were gave me a boisterous welcome.

'I'm looking for whoever dragged me out,' I said.

Nobby Baynes displayed a cheerful grin.

'We'll chalk it up to the squadron if you insist. What about coming with us and having a drink?'

It would have been churlish to refuse. Anton joined the party, and we spent the next half-hour in a ground-floor room which had been turned into a bar. It quickly grew apparent that shooting was not suspected, and my clumsiness on the ice was blamed for the adventure. I breathed a sigh of relief.

They were a jolly crowd, a large proportion of the men being Canadians and Australians, while there were one or two Polish and Free French pilots.

It was while I looked round, after my second and last glass of beer, that an idea assailed me. I drank up swiftly, and left amid a chorus of good-humoured advice, hurrying through the wide stone passages and up the staircase to Cris's room.

He had changed into uniform and was just putting the final touch to his tie.

'Hallo, Ned,' he said cheerfully. 'Duty done? How much did they make you drink?'

I was in no mood for pleasantries.

'I've just had a swine of an idea,' I told him. 'It occurred to me that there's a pretty mixed bag of chaps here, Cris. One of them could have done that shooting, couldn't he? Or am I completely deranged?'

8

I Attend a Secret Conclave

Cris finished arranging his tie, and turned to face me.

'No, you're sane enough,' he said quietly. 'Only a bit late with the idea. I made a quick count of everyone on the lake. There were twenty-one. Two others were in bed, I've checked that with the servants, and three weren't there, or I didn't see them.' He took out his cigarette case. 'I had a word with Nobby Baynes, and he's checking them up as far as he can. He knows they were missing.'

I lit a cigarette and felt at once foolish and worried.

'If we're right about the reason for the shooting,' I said, 'whoever knows that I'm the Voice might know that I come here for weekends. The whole thing could have been done by appointment. What kind of qualification does your mother want before she takes in a convalescent?'

'Sick leave and wings,' said Cris. 'The wings can be reduced to uniform if there aren't too many candidates, but the sick leave is essential. No one not actually in

the R.A.F. can get here, Ned, if that's what you're thinking. In general you're right, though. It could have been
planned to happen here. What else is troubling you?' he
added.

'I wish Clyde wasn't coming,' I said. 'If the sharpshooter is on the premises, he might have a shot at someone who really matters.'

'If he has another try it will be at you primarily,' Cris
said. 'Clyde's voice isn't yours.'

'Oh, nonsense. His organising ability and influence . . .'

'There's one thing you must realise to get a full idea
of your importance at the moment,' said Cris patiently,
'and that's the indubitable fact that your *voice* is the
potent factor. Now what?' he added.

'It will keep,' I said decisively, for the idea which had
come to me was too nebulous to discuss even with him.

Before he had time to press the question the gong went
for lunch. At least, he allowed it to prevent him; had he
really wished, I don't doubt that he could have forced the
idea out of me. As it was we went downstairs at once,
finding the St. Clare family already there. Sheila was
entering as I bowed to her mother.

Lady St. Clare is so much the 'type' which the stage
and cinema have created in the minds of the public that
there were times when I had to look at her hard to make
sure that she was real. A tall woman, with the high-
bridged nose of an aristocrat, she was very much the
grande dame, and the dominant partner.

Towards me she was gracious, but faintly disapprov-
ing.

'I hope you have fully recovered from your immersion,
Mr. Deane.' She smiled pleasantly enough. 'Skating is
not, perhaps, the Englishman's *forte*, do you think?'

'It isn't this Englishman's,' I said with feeling.

'Apparently not.' She turned to her husband. 'Hubert, what time did you say we have to be at the Clarices' this afternoon?'

'Just after three, m'dear.'

'It's too bad I can't come,' said Sheila.

I had already gathered that she disliked the Clarices. A family with a tradition nearly as great as the St. Clares', they lived some ten miles on the other side of Dorchester. I suspected that Sheila had deliberately waited until we were at lunch before making that statement, and facing her mother's glance of surprised disapproval.

There followed a peculiar kind of argument. Probably every fifth sentence Lady St. Clare used was addressed to Sheila, by way of comment, direction, disapproval and, towards the end of the meal, oblique command. Sheila fenced expertly, and I was quite sure that she would not go to the Clarices'.

Nor did she. Her eyes were brimming with fun when the door finally closed.

'Pop's going to tell her that she really *can't* dispose of my life for me, bless him,' she said. 'I say, what's happened to Anton?'

'He was kept at the bar,' I said. 'I saw him deep in conversation with two Frenchmen. Probably they invited him to lunch in the mess.'

'Would they?' Sheila sounded doubtful.

'We could find out,' said Cris. He moved to a nearby telephone, and picked up the receiver. 'Give me the West Wing,' he said to the girl who looked after the private exchange in the estate manager's office. Then he inquired for Anton, and added: 'If you wouldn't mind, yes.' He put a hand over the mouthpiece. 'They think he left some time back, but they're going to make sure.'

For the first time I began to feel worried about Anton. Obviously Sheila shared my anxieties. There were several things that I wanted to ask Cris but thought it wiser that Sheila should not know, so that I was in the invidious position of wanting to look at her, while at the same time hoping that she would soon go.

'All right, thanks.' Cris replaced the receiver thoughtfully. He was frowning. 'He's not there,' he told us.

'Perhaps he's found a clue,' I said half-jocularly.

'Perhaps it isn't so funny,' retorted Sheila rather too tartly. 'I wish I hadn't to go out.' She looked at the clock above the mantelpiece. 'It's five to two, I must go.'

Cris opened the door for her.

'Where are you going, Shee? Far enough from the Clarices?'

'Ten miles in the opposite direction,' said Sheila, 'and if you must know I'm going to address a Women's Institute on why no one should have a big brother in the R.A.F.' She grimaced at him and hurried out. I eyed Cris a little moodily.

'I hope she'll be all right,' I said.

'You're getting the jitters,' Cris accused me, and then added quietly: 'So am I. Ned, there's one good and hard reason why Sheila mustn't know what's happened, or who you are. She'll be safer that way.'

'My God!' I said. 'Cris, you don't seriously think that? No one can be sure whether she knows or not. I—but no, damn it, this is getting out of hand.'

Cris shrugged.

'Let's not exaggerate. All the same, I'd like to know where Anton is. I think I'll ask Nobby to look for him.'

He was stepping towards the door as he spoke, but I stood by it with my hands in my pockets, a stubborn mood possessing me and probably showing on my face.

'That's twice you've mentioned Nobby,' I said. 'Why pick on him?'

'Because he's flown with me and Anton several times,' Cris said briefly. 'Hold yourself on a tight rein, Ned. Clyde will probably clear up a lot of little mysteries for you. I can't.'

I had to let it go at that, but I was moody, puzzled and not a little worried as I went up to my room. I looked out of the window, not because I felt like surveying the white-clad fields and trees, but because Sheila would be going along the drive in a few minutes. I heard the engine of her car, and looked downwards. She was driving round the house, and suddenly glanced up at me. She smiled and waved. My heart turned a somersault, and all my obsessions were flung to the background.

But only for a time. They swept back again.

The Voice, I thought, must have been the reason for the attack. Cris was right there. I saw that there might be other attempts. There was the possibility, too, that Anton had met with some misadventure, and since he obviously knew my job it could be connected. My imagination ran riot, but not in gay colours; it was drab and depressing, shutting out even the memory of Sheila's smile and wave.

I was glad when my telephone rang, and Cris spoke.

'Clyde's here, Ned. Will you come to my room?'

'Yes,' I said briskly. 'I'll be there in two minutes.'

I rang off, but my promise was over-optimistic, for before I had left the room a tap was followed by Nobby Bayne's fair head. Nobby has a cherubic smile, merry blue eyes and an odd faculty for pulling his face into all manner of expressions.

'Sorry to butt in,' he said, 'but Cris told me to see you if he wasn't downstairs. He's not, so here I am.'

'I'm just going to see him,' I said. I repressed my

curiosity despite an urge to ask questions, wondering whether he had yet been asked to look for Anton.

'I'm here to let you know that two or three of our boys saw Duval legging it towards the pond after he left us. We're pursuing inquiries.' Nobby registered a sleuth-on-the-trail expression, and I smiled despite myself. 'About the other business, though. Two of the missing men have turned up; they've been in the village. Friends are staying at the local, I gathered. The other's still missing, a bloke named Lepré. Free French, no one likes him. Pass it on, will you?' Nobby put a hand to his lips to exhort silence, opened the door stealthily and crept out.

I hurried to Cris's room.

Originally, I believe, the room was the vast, private dining-hall of the St. Clares. It was now divided into three rooms, study, bedroom and dressing-room.

In the first room Clyde was sitting in an easy chair. With him was a man I knew slightly, but was surprised to see there: Bannister, the Under-Secretary for Economic Warfare, a thin, pallid-faced man, caustic in criticism, but reputed to be loyal and dependable to his friends.

Cris was standing with his back to the fire.

I apologised for being late, and added hurriedly that there was something Cris needed to know. I told him all that Nobby had told me, and his lips tightened when he heard that Lepré was still missing.

Clyde pushed his chair back and stood up.

'Ned, I'm damnably sorry about this. It's my fault, I should have checked everything here thoroughly.'

I stared at him in surprise, and he went on:

'Had I known Lepré was here I would have had him out quickly. He's been suspect for some time, and we've been watching him. There isn't much doubt who did that shooting. He had a perfect opportunity, and no one, seeing him walking about the grounds, would have reason to suspect him.'

'But why should anyone be suspected?' I asked. 'It doesn't seem reasonable that I should have been deliberately attacked.'

'Reasonable!' Clyde laughed without humour. 'Sooner or later it was inevitable.' He did not enlarge on this astonishing statement, but went on: 'We'll make sure that it doesn't happen again, anyhow, although you'll have to have company wherever you go.'

'Oh, surely not,' I said irritably. 'We don't have to dramatise the thing. And we certainly don't want to exaggerate my importance. That's what you're doing, you know.'

Bannister interrupted, his tone thin and precise.

'You're quite wrong, Deane. Let us have the facts right. I have had reports by the hundred emphasising the importance of the Voice.'

'That's as maybe,' I said, 'but there must be a hundred men in England expert enough at voice imitation, and anyone could speak into the mike with my voice and deceive ninety-nine per cent of the listeners, if not more.'

Bannister looked up sharply, and for a moment I thought that the idea was entirely fresh to them. Clyde cleared his throat.

'I'm glad you thought of that,' he said. 'Bannister and I were talking about it on the way down. Now that the danger is under our nose, we can see it. We can get one or two men to act as impersonators, Ned. You've no objection to letting them listen to you while you get about, to pick up the tone and inflections?'

'Of course not,' I said.

Nevertheless I felt a cold wave of apprehension sweep

over me. I was making admissions to myself by degrees, finding the whole too much to accept at one sitting. Probably the cumulative effect was worse than if I had taken a deep breath and gulped it down at once.

The shooting spelt danger; in all probability there would be other attempts. Believing this, Clyde and Bannister had seen the need for having an understudy, or two or three understudies, in case I was disposed of. Even when it came from a good friend and a more than kindly mentor, the tacit declaration that I was not safe had little to commend it. I had thought of the impersonation idea—in case I fell ill, or was away for any other reason. Or so I had convinced myself; now I admitted that it was really in case I was murdered.

Clyde went on to say that they had come down to save me the trouble of visiting London, but that did not satisfy me, and I pressed for an amplification, hinting that there were mysteries concerning Cris and Anton which were already half-admitted, and that I felt the circumstances demanded a full revelation. I saw Clyde look at Bannister, and realised that the Under-Secretary had come to handle any such eventuality; later I suspected that Cris had warned Clyde that I was not likely to be easily satisfied.

'I think I can answer your questions,' Bannister began. 'In the first place . . .'

That was as far as he got before the door opened abruptly and Sheila burst into the room, her face white and tense. I had never seen her like it before, and the revelation took my mind off Bannister's words completely.

She stood before us, her back to the door, looking from one to the other; and then said clearly:

'Anton's been murdered. I've sent for the police.'

9

To Die or Not?

Sheila had been driving past the place where the sharpshooter had waited for me near the pond. She had looked
towards it, then seen something which had made her get
out and hurry across the wooded patch of land. Anton's
service hat had been lying amongst the trees; near it a
trail of blood lay on the white rime frost.

This she had followed, coming upon Anton with an
ugly wound in his neck.

The nearest doctor was in St. Clare village, two miles
further on. She had left Anton and hurried to the doctor,
bringing him back to the spot. Then she had rushed to
the house and telephoned the Dorchester police.

'They're sending someone here at once,' Sheila finished
abruptly. 'I knew it was crazy not to report the shooting
in the first instance. If we had done that, Anton might
now be alive.'

'Easy, Shee,' said Cris, getting up and going to her.
'No one had any reason for thinking Anton was in danger,
you know. And we weren't our own masters.'

'I think your sister should know that the instructions
not to advise the police of any eventuality until we had
been consulted came from us,' Bannister said drily.

Sheila's expression remained unchanged.

'Dr. Peverell will of course bring Anton here,' Cris
said. 'I'd better go downstairs.'

I remember being vaguely surprised that both Clyde
and Bannister followed him.

I was left in Cris's room with Sheila, who was close to tears, and the sickening belief that Anton was dead and that we might have saved him. It left me with nothing to say, and awkwardly I put a hand on her shoulder. I was remembering vividly Anton's confession of love for her; I wondered whether he had spoken of it to her, but I knew one thing which transcended all others, although just then it gave me no joy.

I was in love with Sheila.

'I wonder . . .' I said, and stopped. Then I went to the telephone and rang Jameson. 'Send up tea for one—no, two—to this room, Jameson, please.'

I rang off to see Sheila smiling at me. It was a rather dismal smile, but a genuine one nevertheless.

'Bless you, Ned,' she said. 'You're so gloriously normal. Tea, of course, I can do with it, too.' She began to talk nervously, quickly, with a brittle urgency which made her words difficult to follow.

Apparently Anton's failure to arrive at lunch had worried her because of the shooting, which had already put her on edge. For Anton to come out of France as he had, to escape all the danger and horrors there, only to be murdered when he had every reason to feel secure, was too horrible to contemplate with detachment.

'Where is it going to stop?' she asked wildly. 'You're in danger though you won't admit it, and you must have expected something like this. Ned, you didn't tell me the truth when you said you'd no idea, did you?'

She paused for the first time, staring at me wide-eyed.

'If I can't tell you the whole truth about everything or anything, Sheila,' I said slowly, 'I'll say nothing. I mustn't talk of confidential matters, but at least I needn't lie to you. The whole affair was as great a surprise to me as it was to you. Only when Cris shocked me into thinking, did I realise that the threat could have been there for some time.'

She drew a deep breath. I think she felt happier in her mind; easier, at all events, and I know I was glad that my assurance affected her that way.

'Thanks, Ned,' she said. 'Now I'd better go to my room and repair the ravages. I wish . . .'

I imagined she was going to say that she wished she knew what was happening downstairs. So did I. We were both sufficiently on edge to jump when the telephone rang.

It was Cris.

'There's a chance for Anton,' he said without preamble. 'He's being put in the ambulance now, and an operation might save him. I'm going with him. Clyde and Bannister will be in the library when you're through.'

He closed down abruptly, while I hardly heard the latter part of his words.

'There's a chance for Anton,' I said as she started to speak. 'He's not dead.'

'Oh, thank God!' exclaimed Sheila.

She sat down on the nearest chair and began to cry.

Jameson, the soul of tact, came in with the tray, placed it quietly on a table, and went out, while I stared at the tray and then at Sheila. Suddenly I thought the most obvious, everyday thing would be the best, and I went over to the table and picked up the teapot.

'Try this, Shee,' I said a few seconds later, using the affectionate diminutive which I had heard only Cris use before.

Her paroxysm was nearing its end. I stood like a dumbit, holding two cups of tea, wondering what the blazes I would do if she did not stop. For the first time in my life I was literally tongue-tied.

71

Sheila straightened up and pushed her hair back from her face; she was smiling. It was a strange moment, and in spite of the tears and her red eyes, she looked so good that I drew in a sharp involuntary breath. Her hand was a little unsteady as she stretched out for the tea, saying in a tear-drenched voice:

'Iron-nerved Sheila unmasked at last. Ned, I don't think I've ever let anyone else see me cry. Can you keep secrets?'

'I can keep this one,' I said with relief. 'Look here, would you like a lacing of whisky in that?'

She was stirring the tea absently, although she does not take sugar.

'No, darling, I'm all right,' she said.

I nearly dropped my cup. I darted a single glance at her, but she was drinking with eyes half-closed. I do not know whether she meant the 'darling', or whether it slipped out as a casual endearment. I took a sip of tea quickly, finding it too hot. I gasped and nearly dropped the cup for a second time, tears springing to my eyes.

'Are you going to make a pair of us?' Sheila asked.

She was alluding to the tears, of course, but the other association of 'make a pair' sprang immediately to my mind. I would not have been surprised had I blurted out a proposal there and then, and I might have done so but for the noise above me.

I have little to be grateful for towards the man who made that noise, but on that one occasion I think it certain that he saved me from making a fool of myself.

Sheila glanced upwards with an involuntary: 'What's that?'

At the same moment we saw a shadow against the glass roof-light.

It was a shadow something like you would see on the

opposite side of a frosted-glass panel, except that being above our heads it was impossible to discern any kind of shape.

Crack! The sound came again.

I had a swift impression of a man wielding a hammer, and I jumped to Sheila, dragging her to one side. Both the cups fell to the floor, their crash synchronising with the third *crack!* from above.

'Out!' I snapped. 'Hurry!'

Sheila went as far as the door while I lifted the house telephone, calling the exchange. I forced myself to speak quietly and without, I hoped, causing undue alarm.

'There is someone on the roof of the central wing,' I said. 'Tell Jameson and McReady to have the house surrounded at once. Do you understand me?'

'Yes, sir,' said a self-possessed voice, and the line went dead.

The glass broke then, but it did not splinter.

Several white lines appeared to spring from a central hole. Beyond it the shadow was moving. Wishing that I had a gun I stepped towards Sheila. Then a piece of rounded metal was thrust into the hole.

'God!' I exclaimed. 'A grenade!'

I swung round and plunged through the door to Cris's bedroom, carrying Sheila with me, my one thought to keep her covered.

The explosion when it came was not loud.

The door proved a protection against the blast, although I felt it plainly enough. I scrambled to my feet swiftly. Then I thought of the possibility of another attempt, and lifted Sheila across the room to the other side of the four-poster bed.

But for that I might have been able to get the fire under control.

Until I had put Sheila down I did not notice the flames, but when I reached the door of the study the fire was burning fiercely, with the intense white flame which only magnesium can give. I thought 'incendiary' automatically, and grabbed a cushion from the nearest chair, but I was too late to prevent the second explosion. It was just as well that I was too late; had I been a couple of yards nearer, I would in all probability have been seriously, if not fatally, injured.

There was no hope now of putting out the fire unaided. A dozen smaller outbreaks had sprung up, one beside the bookcases, a second by the door, another by the fireplace.

'The door,' I whispered. 'I must put that one out.'

I leapt forward in an attempt to do so, when I saw Sheila by my side.

'Where's the nearest extinguisher?' I asked her. I put more heartiness into my voice than was genuine, as I pulled at the handle.

I pulled twice again before I realised that the door was locked, and several seconds passed before I knew the key must have been turned deliberately on the outside.

10

In Which My Mind Really
Becomes Unsettled

The room was filled with smoke by then: the grey, acrid smoke with which London had become so familiar. The original stone floor had been covered with parquet blocks, and these were burning in some places, while the side of the room where the books had been was a roaring mass of flames. The noise, the smoke and the realisation that we were locked in might well have confused me, but I was clear-headed enough. Sheila peered at me through a misty veil of smoke; she was only a few seconds after me in realising what was the matter.

We turned away from the door together.

The fire had not yet reached the bedroom, but smoke was coiling about the ceiling and seeping through the wooden partition, which I knew would collapse very soon. Sheila was going on to the smaller room, but I grabbed her arm.

'This way,' I said.

I stripped the top blanket and sheet from the bed, while Sheila grabbed the rest of the bedclothes. As she did so there was a rumbling sound, not loud enough for a crash but very near it. The partition had caved in, and the flames shot ten or fifteen feet into the room. They caught a corner of one of Sheila's sheets. She stamped it out swiftly, and we staggered choking and gasping into the outer room.

We closed the door behind us swiftly, and then leaned against it, retching and gasping for breath. Tears were streaming down my cheeks, and I could not see Sheila clearly.

Madly I tried to work out some means of escape.

The outer door of Cris's apartment had been made to withstand assault by fire and steel and battering ram. I knew that whoever had turned the key in the lock would not have left it there for anyone to turn again; that key was gone, and before the door could be forced down Sheila and I would be dead.

St. Clare House, in its medieval days, had been built with an eye to security, as I have said. I knew the wall outside the window well, because from the grounds I had often remarked on its sheer face. There was a drop of something more than thirty feet to the terrace, and no kind of foothold. There was no chance at all of climbing down the wall without the aid of a ladder or a rope, and I had no means of being sure that the general alarm had yet been raised.

The sheets and blankets offered the only hope of escape.

Hastily we began to knot them together, one length of sheet to one of blanket, so that we had an over-all length of something like twenty feet; that left little to spare.

My heart sank when I looked about the room.

I should have known, of course, but I had forgotten; the furniture there was small and light. There was nothing heavy enough to take the weight of Sheila, and my eleven stone-odd would obviously prove far too much for anything we could use as an anchor. Two armchairs were the most likely pieces, and Sheila moved towards one.

'No use,' I said. 'Let's get the window open.'

76

It had some kind of a patent fastener, and we worked at it for several seconds before loosening it. When at last it swung open I could see several people hurrying away from the house. I tried to shout, but my voice was too hoarse to carry.

My God, I thought, they'll never be in time.

'Perhaps they've gone for a ladder,' Sheila said. 'They must know what's happening.'

'Of course,' I said quickly, 'but we'll beat them to it. Get hold of this.'

We were standing very near to one another, our faces closer than they had ever been.

'Ned, oughtn't you to go first? You're the most important . . .'

'Don't waste time,' I said sharply. 'Can you keep a firm hold on this?'

'Yes. But, Ned . . .'

'Don't argue!' I snapped, and pushed the end of the blanket into her hand. She gripped it, twisting it round one wrist. Once she saw that I was quite decided on what to do, she was quick enough, resting her free hand against the window sill as she climbed over.

For some seconds she was kneeling on the sill, trying to get a firmer hold. If she felt dizzy or nervous, she did not show it, although she must have known that a single slip would be disastrous.

All this had taken time; not much, perhaps, but enough for those accursed flames to devour the bedroom and to be shooting through the holes they had charred in the second partition. Smoke was pouring through the window then, one gust so sudden and thick that Sheila completely disappeared.

I experienced a moment of sheer terror, thinking she had dropped.

Then the smoke cleared, showing that she was still kneeling on the sill, but beginning to lower herself. I took a firm grasp of the blanket about three feet away from her, and began to let it out slowly.

Sheila weighs less than ten stone, but her weight on the end of that rope was incredible. As she disappeared from my sight, I felt that I could not hold on. The sheet—I had passed the first knot—was cutting at my hands, as her full weight hung from it. I tightened my grip again, and lowered inch by inch, clenching my teeth.

I did not expect to get away.

The smoke was choking me and breathing was almost impossible. That was bad enough, but the heat on my back was worse. I could not see the flames, but there was a red glow about me and I could hear the fire crackling quite close to my ears.

I felt no particular fear; I was concentrating too much on Sheila's safe descent. While the weight remained on me I knew she was all right.

Abruptly it eased.

I staggered forward against the window, without strength or substance, gasping for air. My breathing grew more than a torture; it became a laboured, wheezing thing, allowing a trickle of air to pass down my throat. I suppose I was on the point of losing consciousness when a figure loomed out of the smoke in front of me.

I did not recognise Cris. He said afterwards that he spoke to me but that I did not answer; that is not surprising, for I heard nothing but the fire and the whirling, droning sound of the smoke in my head, going round and round.

I felt myself lifted from my feet, and then appeared to be suspended in mid-air. Actually I was on Cris's back, and he was already feeling his way down the ladder which had been run up to the window.

I stopped moving. There were voices, some close, some far away. One of them was so near that I heard the words:

'Take it easy, Shee, he's all right.'

I thought I heard a sob, and knew Cris had spoken. Then I found myself on my back, and there was a strange, agonising pressure beneath my ribs.

'He'll do,' someone said.

A long time after that I found myself in my own room. Hazily I supposed I was back at Clyde's house after my return from France. The next time I opened my eyes Cris was there.

'Taken by and large, Ned, you're not feeling too bad?'

'Not bad at all,' I said. 'By George, it wasn't a good spell, but—Cris! How's Sheila?'

'She's all right,' he said quietly. 'She fainted after we'd brought you down. She isn't as scorched as you, and she did come down mostly clad,' he added with a smile. 'You were in rags and as near mother-naked as I've ever seen you!'

I stared at him.

'No joke,' he assured me. 'Your clothes had charred pretty badly, I suppose, and they just dropped to pieces as I carried you down.'

'*You* carried me down. Cris, I ...'

'Now look here,' said Cris firmly, 'we aren't indulging in any presentation of verbal laurels. So forget it. If I hadn't, someone else would have. Do you think you can walk across the room?'

'I know I can,' I said, and stood up. I staggered round the bed, then sat on it with slow dignity. My head was giddy, but otherwise I was not too bad. 'You see,' I boasted. 'I'm perfectly all right. I—here, what's the light on for?'

'It's nearly six,' Cris went on. 'What do you make of it, Ned? How did it start?'

I told him, but before I was halfway through he interrupted.

'I think I know the rest. The girl at the exchange didn't lose much time, and we had the place surrounded pretty quickly. We would have been with you much earlier, but the swine managed to lock up the shed where we keep the ladders, and it took some time to break the door down.'

'Who was it?'

'Lepré. He saw that we had him surrounded, and started a race across the roof. He climbed the main tower, with Nobby and two of the others after him.'

'Go on,' I urged. I saw the tower in my mind's eye, soaring upward as high as a church steeple.

'Lepré slipped,' Cris said briefly. 'The one positive tragedy of the day.'

I gulped; that tower was all of three hundred feet high, with a sheer drop to the flagged courtyard below.

'We wanted to him to talk,' Cris went on, 'but that finished that. We don't know a lot more than we did at first, although we can piece some things together. Anton . . .'

'He's all right?'

'Operation successful,' Cris assured me. 'He's on the danger list, of course, but . . .'

'Weren't you going with him?'

'I came back,' Cris said. His smile told me a lot more than his words, and he went on: 'He'd seen Lepré hiding in a gamekeeper's hut, talking to another man. He went after them, and they met him halfway. The idiot didn't have a gun with him, instead of hurrying for help he decided that he could handle them. Still, the report from the hospital is much better than I expected it would be, and we're not going to grumble. Ned, can you face Clyde and Bannister for half an hour? There are some things they want to talk about.'

I said grimly: 'There are some things I want to talk about, too. Bring 'em here.'

Cris chuckled as he went out, and I reflected on all that he had told me. Although it was not until the following day that I heard anything more about Garat's attack on me, this is probably the best place to record it.

Lepré had reached the roof without difficulty from the dormitory wing of the 'Home'. It was evident that he had reconnoitred the position carefully, and that he knew the glass roof of Cris's room. It's clear, too, that he was in the central part of the house, for the possibility of there being an accomplice was dismissed after a full investigation. The theory is that he was watching Cris's room from the stone spiral staircase which leads from it to the roof, saw us all go in there, saw Cris and the others leave, slipped down and, after Jameson's arrival, locked the doors and took the key away. Finally he had returned to the roof to smash a way through the glass and put paid to me.

He failed because of the toughened glass. My warning over the telephone had prevented his escape, and in his desperation to avoid capture he had slipped to his death; there was no more to it than that, although perhaps I should say, no less.

It was while I was waiting for Cris and the others that I realised that I had asked no question about the fire. I waited until he had ushered Bannister and Clyde in, and then said sharply:

'Cris, how much damage?'

'It didn't spread any further than the stone walls,' Cris reassured me. He turned to Clyde. 'Curious specimen of a man they can't kill.'

'Nevertheless I've been closer to being killed than I like,' I said, eyeing Clyde suspiciously.

Bannister had said nothing until then. Perhaps he would have maintained his silence had not Clyde glanced towards him.

The air was taut with expectancy. Something of importance was coming, although I had no idea what it was. My mind worked swiftly, and I decided that I should soon know the real reason for the visit of Clyde and Bannister. As the Voice I might carry some weight, but as Norman Deane, of F2 at the B.B.C., I was certainly not important enough for Clyde and Bannister to visit me, even after the shooting. Clyde on his own would not have been surprising; it was Bannister's arrival which puzzled me.

'I am not at all sure that we are wise to discuss it to-night,' Bannister said in his dry, precise voice. 'Can we reasonably expect Deane to reach a sound and unbalanced judgement of the issues involved?'

'Try him, sir,' said Cris.

By that time I was on edge, and spoke more testily perhaps than I knew.

'Look here, I don't mind being shot at if it has to happen, and a hand-grenade more or less makes little difference, but I'm damned if I can see why this mystery is necessary. If you've a proposition, let me hear it. You were beginning to tell me how Cris and Anton knew my job. Is that anything to do with it?'

'Yes,' said Bannister almost before I had finished. 'St. Clare and Duval are two of several pilots who make regular visits to occupied France, Deane. They make

82

contact with Free French sympathisers there. In fact, they follow up the contacts you make by radio.'

I goggled at him.

I knew, mind you, that occasionally one of our planes landed in France and picked up sympathisers; I did not know that the code messages I put over the radio actually made those appointments; and I had not dreamed that Cris and Anton were in any way involved.

I said weakly: 'Well I'm damned!'

Bannister went on as if I had not spoken.

'A regular service from England to France has been running for some time, Deane. The scope of it hardly concerns you. It could be much wider, and we hope that eventually it will be. One of the results, of course, is that we have learned just how effective your broadcasts have been in France, and we had information some time ago that agents had been sent to this country to first identify and then remove the Voice. Your identity was known to very few, you yourself did not know the meaning of the messages you sent to our agents in France. The danger seemed slight; we now know that it is considerable.'

'Yes,' I said, feeling far more unsettled in my mind than I could ever remember.

'We feel now,' Bannister continued dispassionately, 'that we can make another move to unsettle the German forces in France. Much of what we are doing, and you are doing, has a practical value. We get good men into the Free French forces, we learn information about the effect of the blockade and general conditions in France. But there is another aspect. We want to *worry* the German Government. We are already doing so in a small degree admittedly, but we want to double, treble, our nuisance value.'

'Yes, yes,' I said. 'But where is all this leading to?'

Clyde said quietly: 'All right, Bannister, I'll finish. Ned, your influence while speaking from England is considerable. Your influence, *speaking in France*, would be far greater. The Huns would really have something to worry about then—imagine an English transmitter actually in occupied France!—and the French would be consolidated, would feel our influence much closer to them. We haven't done more than outline the situation, but it has been accepted that you would be far more valuable in France than in England. It must be you, or your voice—something the French have learned to know and to trust. So we want you to go there.'

II

I am Groomed for Espionage of a New Kind

All manner of objections to Clyde's suggestion sprang into my mind. For one thing I could not fully accept the importance of my voice. For another, the practical difficulties appeared to be insoluble. To have a transmitting station in occupied territory was no small task. I thought then that transmitting messages to be picked up by the ordinary receiving set was a complicated business and that a small army of engineers and all manner of complicated equipment was necessary; at least that was how it was at the station from which I regularly spoke. I am not an engineer, and the whole system of trapping the vocal oscillations on the other end is to me a mystery as complete as the method of counteracting magnetic mines.

Those objections, and others far more trivial, sprang to my mind, but I can say with honesty that personal danger had no part in them. I did plenty of shrinking afterwards, but it was not my first reaction.

I put some of my thoughts into words, to be cut short by Bannister.

'No, Deane, those factors need not worry you. The arrangements are made, the thing can be done. But there *is* a considerable risk, in fact a very great risk. On the other hand we can call on a number of volunteers, some who are already working in France. The peculiar need is for your voice.'

'I'm beginning to dislike my voice,' I said flippantly.

Cris grinned sympathetically.

'If you decide to go, you'll have contact with me, Anton when he's better, and others from time to time. There are four transmitting stations already prepared, and others will be made. As the Huns get one, you'll hop into another. You'll have a smokescreen about you thicker than the one in my room today. We wouldn't lose that voice for the world! Eh, Sir Alan?'

'You're right,' said Clyde emphatically.

'Deane.' Bannister leaned forward, wagging a forefinger towards me to emphasise his point. His grey eyes were narrow but very compelling. 'This proposition is one which has been well discussed, and you must accept it as established that the work can and will be done. Our only problem is—who shall speak? We want you, because we believe you will have the greatest effect for good on the French, for bad on the Germans. This may not be an appropriate time for discussing it with you, but the issue is important as we are ready to begin operating. I am going to remind you that your country, not Clyde or my-self or St. Clare, is asking this of you.'

That appeal to patriotism, especially from Bannister, was queerly surprising and effective. Not that it was necessary; from the first it had not occurred to me to say 'No' and it did not then. But that did not make me think the prospect any more palatable.

'Take a night to think it over, Ned,' said Clyde. 'We're staying until the morning . . .'

I interrupted almost irritably.

'There's nothing to think over. If you're convinced that I'm the man for the job, then that's all there is to it. I'm a long way from sure that it's going to do much good . . .'

I paused abruptly, for suddenly my objections and my unspoken arguments seemed insignificant. The best brains in the country had doubtless investigated the whole prospect thoroughly. Of course it was practical, of course it was better than working in England.

There was a noticeable easing in the tension. Cris broke the silence which followed with a quiet:

'I told you there was no need to worry, gentlemen. There are a lot of things to arrange, of course, but we needn't go into them now.'

Clyde stood up, and put a hand on my shoulder.

'Thanks, Ned. I should never have thought it would be asking too much of you; but I did.'

'Oh, nonsense,' I said, eager to put an end to this part of it. 'Tell me, how does St. Clare know so much about it?'

Clyde chuckled.

'He's been with us for some time, Ned. You may re-member I once said to you that it was a pity he was with the R.A.F.?'

I nodded.

'Well, I thought more about it, and was able to get him transferred. He's with us.'

'With "us"?'

'F2 is a branch of the Department, no more,' said Clyde. 'We're attached to the Ministry of Economic Warfare.'

'But surely it's Secret Intelligence work?'

'Partly, yes,' Bannister interpolated. 'We have our own agents, Deane. You'll learn all that is necessary during the next week. Don't get your mind too confused now. You've had a trying time.'

'I'm as clear-headed now as I'm ever likely to be,' I said with decision. 'You can at least tell me enough to satisfy the questions I'm bound to ask myself.'

Bannister shrugged.

'Please yourself. You are wondering where my ministry comes into it, of course. France is a reservoir of industrial manpower which the Germans are trying to use. We can stop raw materials going in, and hamper the manufacture of arms the Germans are using, but we cannot prevent the exploitation of raw materials in France and occupied Europe. To judge the full effect of our blockade we must know industrial conditions on the other side. We need to get the French to slow down on production. That task is more ours than any other department, so the particular job we have for you is under our direction, not Secret Intelligence.'

'Which is no more than advisory,' Cris put in.

'Exactly,' said Bannister. 'Is that enough, Deane?'

There were no more insistent questions in my mind, so it had to be enough. Bannister went out, leaving Clyde with Cris and me.

In the general conversation which followed I gathered that Cris and Duval and the small body of pilots who did their dangerous work brought more than men out of France; they brought information.

It was when that dawned on me that I said abruptly: 'Damn it, I can broadcast information to you!'

'Not so dumb, you see,' Cris said, smiling triumphantly. 'Ned, I've been telling them all along that they were seriously underestimating you. Of course you can broadcast information from France to us. We want that more than we want anything else, there's a two-way switch on this thing. But we've already got the men to broadcast home for Bannister's benefit, that's how the idea started. The process will go into operation next week.'

'Why the devil didn't you say so before?' I grumbled.

The fact that information could be transmitted by radio to *England* was a concrete thing, an advantage over everything else, and a far stronger inducement to me than anything Bannister had put up. That was my first intimation of Bannister's honesty. They did not want me to broadcast to England; anyone could do that. They wanted me to broadcast to France; and he believed only I could do it effectively at that juncture.

Someone rang for Clyde, who left Cris and me together. I felt suddenly that I needed to see Sheila.

'What are you going to do for dinner?' Cris asked. 'Are you coming down?'

I was torn two ways, and asked: 'Is Sheila?'

'No.'

'Then I think I'll stay here,' I said. 'Can you have it with me?'

'Not very well,' Cris said reasonably, 'with Bannister and Clyde downstairs I'd better show up. What do you feel like? Dinner or a snack?'

'Oh, nothing heavy,' I said hastily.

He went off, and I felt very much on my own. I dwelt

little on what Clyde and Bannister had asked and, what was more, my new undertaking. Each time any thought entered my head about that I shied from it, and concentrated on Sheila having dinner in her room, and me in mine, separated by a few walls and a host of conventions and thinking how damn silly it was. In fact it would not have been difficult for me to work myself into a fine state of indignation over it.

A tap on the door startled me. I glanced up, and there was Sheila.

I looked at her, trying to keep the love and longing out of my face, enormously relieved to see that she showed no traces of the fire.

'I can't believe it,' she said. 'Cris told me you were all right, but I thought he was putting me off. Aren't you hurt *any*where?' Her eyes searched my face.

'Everywhere, but not enough to attract the sympathy I deserve,' I said promptly. 'Shec, I've just been telling myself it was darned silly for you to eat alone and me to eat alone.'

She approached me slowly.

'Ned, I don't know what to say. You were . . .' She broke off, turning her head away.

I could have prolonged the moment indefinitely, but I thought it fairer to her not to do so. I patted her hand and said gently: 'The child must eat. I'll tell Jameson to bring you something here.'

I busied myself by telephoning Jameson, and moving tables about, until Sheila's voice became less emotional.

She said at last with a show of gaiety: 'I've just had three things dinned into me. (a) Don't ask questions. (b) Don't ask questions. (c) Don't ask questions. So you see I'm properly broken in.'

I chuckled with relief, for I had been wondering how

I could evade the subject of Clyde and Bannister's visit. As it was I did tell her that I had been posted to a new job, and might not be in the country all the time. At the realisation that I would see her only very occasionally, my heart dropped.

Sheila nodded wisely.

'I thought something was brewing. Are you going to America?' she added abruptly.

'Who knows? I'll be here and there and everywhere, Shee.'

Jameson arrived with our trays at this point, and we chatted lightheartedly over an excellent meal.

No one arrived until ten o'clock.

Looking back, it was the most contented and completely enjoyable two hours I had had in my life until then. Never once did we talk of our escape or our own danger, and it was surprising how easily we discussed subjects with a range wider than I had suspected I knew, not exactly with a personal touch but with that quiet, comfortable restfulness which very occasionally inspires companionship. I could have gone on for hours, talking or listening, and noticing as the evening wore on how her hair, which she had obviously washed, grew fluffy and nearer to its normal shade and intriguing unruliness.

When Cris came in we said good night, and Sheila slipped away.

Cris was moving into the next room to mine for the night. There was an intercommunicating door which we unlocked, but before long he was getting no answers to his comments. I was fast asleep. I remained like that until I was awakened by a hand on my shoulder.

Vaguely, I recognised Cris.

'Too bad to get you up so early,' he said, 'but we're on the move, Ned.'

I struggled up as he switched on the main light. He was fully dressed, in uniform, and smiling at my bewilderment.

'London, my boy, and right away.'

'But damn it, what's the time?' I looked at my watch. 'Five past six! What *is* this?'

'You're leaving here before light,' said Cris. 'We don't want any more sharpshooting episodes. How are you feeling?'

'I'm all right,' I said. Obviously there was no room for further argument.

'Breakfast will be up in twenty minutes,' he told me, 'and we leave at seven.'

'I—here, does Sheila know?'

'No. Only Clyde and Bannister.'

'Blast it!' I said with feeling.

Cris himself brought me breakfast, and I was finished and ready at ten minutes to seven. I then sat down to write a line to Sheila. Facing a sheet of paper, I grew aghast at the difficulty of beginning.

Finally, when I had wasted six minutes in fruitless thought, I seized a pen and wrote:

I've been dragged out by that unholy brother of yours, and the Lord knows when I'll be back. I'll phone you from London or wherever I get to, and look in if it's only for an hour before I go off to wherever I go! Regards to Anton—nurse him carefully!

Yours, Ned.

I put her name on an envelope, sealed it, and left it on the dressing-table. By then Cris was back, and we went downstairs, leaving the house by one of the side doors. Cris had a car waiting, and he took the wheel. It

91

was still pitch dark, and to add to the depression there was a faint drizzle.

For a time Cris drove exceedingly fast, then dropped to a leisurely thirty-five.

'Why that burst of speed, madhead?'

'We could have been followed.'

'Followed? No, damn it . . .'

'Hush,' said Cris, and I could imagine his smile. 'Get it into that thick head of yours, Ned, that you're a badly wanted man, and Hitler has plenty of agents over here prepared to kill you and take a chance of getting away. That's one of the many things you've got to remember. You're in deep.'

There was silence for a while, and then I said: 'Cris, what have you been doing for the past six months? I wish you'd uncover your history a bit. Somehow or other you've got well within the machinations of Clyde and Bannister, you don't just take messages to France and bring others back. Messages or people,' I added, to make sure that he could not be evasive.

What he told me is more than enough for the subject matter of another book. The trouble is that only he could tell it, for the bald outlines that he gave me needed etching in with detail and that he will never do. I am glad that after the adventure at St. Clare House I was with him often enough to be able to write this one and, if I live, others to follow. The career of Crispian St. Clare is a remarkable, even an incredible, history.

I know the inspiration of it. It is strange to think that Cris, most kindly, generous, lovable and gentle of men, should be actuated by hate; but hatred guided him, led him, upheld him, and saw him through his dangers. It was hatred of everything and anything German.

Now and again it reveals itself in all its nakedness.

It is a terrible thing, and sometimes frightening, but some-how, in Cris, it never seems wrong even in its harshest manifestation. It was not exactly vengeance; at least, not vengeance for himself. The occasional half-confidence he gave me from time to time made it clear that the Battle of France, and what he learned while he was there, saw the birth of it.

After reporting to his own base with me and the *poilus* and going back for others whom Duval collected in the clearing, Cris had learned from Duval what he had sus-pected before, the rottenness of much of the French Army, particularly in the senior ranks. He had gathered also that there were many thoroughly reliable officers.

Starting with the idea which he had expressed to me, Clyde had made arrangements by which Cris, and others, became Special Branch agents, not directly responsible to the R.A.F. One after another he had brought men from France to join de Gaulle, some important, some just men of France who would not suffer the Nazi heel. There had been several occasions, he told me, when he had been nearly caught, others when he had been forced to take a long and dangerous detour to get his men out of the grip of the Nazis who had arrested them.

What Cris did not tell me was that he had contrived to get results far beyond those of anyone else, that he rarely failed to take his toll of the Nazis in the neighbour-hood where he was operating. I learned much of that afterwards, from Nobby and Anton and the seven or eight other pilots whom I came to know well.

Cris eventually had become a kind of liaison officer be-tween F2 (Air Strength) and Clyde and Bannister; that explained his familiarity with them, and the confidence they obviously reposed in him.

By the time he had finished telling me all this, we were entering London.

For the first time I discovered that Cris had been so sure that I would join in with the project that all preparations had been made.

The first shock I had was going into an office in Whitehall and seeing a man stand up from a desk and turn to face me. It was like looking at myself in a mirror when I knew no mirror was there. I stared at him, stupefied, and Cris's quiet chuckle brought me to earth.

'Not bad, eh, Ned? Meet your impersonator.'

'Impersonator?' I said, and then stammered: 'It—it's uncanny.'

Cris told me that my habits, mannerisms, voice and bearing had been studied for weeks, and that a theatrical make-up artist, now with the Secret Intelligence, had worked on my impersonator for several days to get the required likeness. Sheila would not have been deceived, nor anyone who knew me really well; but casual acquaintances could not have told us apart.

I did not ask questions, but gathered that officially I was to remain in England. The other man would come in for any further assaults; I felt sorry for him at first, but after a brief conversation knew that he was aware of the risks and accepted them cheerfully; he was a Secret Intelligence man, loaned to F2. He stayed with me whenever I was indoors during the next five days, but was never seen out of doors with me.

Cris went down to the base, and I visited it while he was there, to meet the other pilots. They were all veterans of the Battle of France, all youngish men, and all bomber-pilots.

Near the base Cris and Clyde, who joined us there, took me into a village conspicuous by the absence of billeted soldiers. They led me to one of the cottages, small and ordinary enough.

'What is all this about?' I demanded, thoroughly mystified.

'We want to get your reaction,' said Cris briefly.

My reaction to that moment was not kindly; but it altered when Cris led the way to a cellar. There was a heap of logs in one corner. A switch must have been pressed, for suddenly they swung away from the wall, showing a dark cavity below. I stood for some seconds with my mouth open, for I might have been entering the announcer's room at F2.

I will not try to go into technical detail about the equipment, beyond saying that there was far more than a microphone. I noticed an instrument panel for listening and recording, and on one wall a section of pigeon-holes for filing notes and comments. There was a cabinet of gramophone records and the gramophone itself, used, I supposed, for playing the national airs of France.

The room was about twelve feet square, and there was hardly a patch of wall without its instruments.

I turned to Cris and Clyde.

'So this is a replica of the places you've built on the other side,' I said.

Cris nodded.

'We've four established over there, cottages and cellars complete. It probably won't be long before the first is found, once you start, and you can move to the next. We'll go on building them, so that you can have a regular change. Three days in one place will be enough, and if we have the luck to escape being located we can use them more than once. If we don't, a touch on a button and everything will be blown sky-high.'

A strange touch that, I thought.

I wandered about the room, handling this instrument and that, feeling my way in a new, unreal world.

'You're broadcasting from here tonight,' Cris said, 'and telling them that you'll be in France tomorrow.'

I nodded, not really surprised, and it was not until we were back at the base that I realised there would be no chance of going to St. Clare House, even for the hour I had promised Sheila. True, I had often wondered whether that promise had been necessary or wise; I had only the companionship of those two hours in my room to judge by, and had been afraid lest she should read presumption in it.

Cris told me of a man named Hewison, with whom I would work on the other side, and gave me a few other details.

My broadcast was timed for half past seven. I finished it with a peculiar feeling of elation, and, let me admit, a feeling also of apprehension. The France I remembered was the devastated France of the Nazi avalanche, with a sullen, defeated, desperate people. I did not let myself brood, however, and Clyde had suggested that Cris and I should go to his house for a late dinner and a mild celebration before leaving for France.

My only interest in the plan was the chance it might give me to telephone Sheila. Clyde and Cris let me go ahead, and opening the lounge door I found Sheila sitting in an easy chair by the fire.

12

I Make a Difficult Decision

When I saw her I stood quite still on the threshold. The picture of her is one which will never fade from my mind's eye, and I conjure it in a flash wherever I am. It has comforted me and cheered me in moments of desperation and despair, boredom and danger. In that strange room, with only a standard lamp behind Sheila's chair and the fire to give light, there was a quality of beauty and contentment which never faded.

Sheila stood up.

My mind began to work more evenly, and my heart stopped thumping. I realised that it was no accident that Clyde and Cris had left me to enter the room on my own. It had been planned; they knew that I was in love with her, and had contrived this deliberately.

But did they know whether Sheila was in love with me?

I thought then, I hoped, that she was. I remembered Anton's 'She is half in love with you already'. Other things entered my mind, too; thoughts of the move into France that was coming, the danger which must inevitably be there, the comparatively slight chance of my getting back to England safely—or perhaps I should say, the negligible possibility that I would live until the war was over. That factor guided me more than anything else. I knew then that in the circumstances I was not justified in asking Sheila to marry me, or accepting her promise if she should agree to do so. I could not, however, stifle my burst of happiness at seeing her.

'Sheila, my dear!' I stepped swiftly towards her and gripped her hands. 'Who waved the magic wand?'

'Cris,' said Sheila. 'He knew that I was in town. Well, Ned?' She looked at me searchingly. 'How are you?'

'If the past week is anything to judge by,' I said, 'I'm going to be sitting pretty until the end of the war. No more lethal attacks, alarms or excursions. Instead I get followed about by a heavy-footed gentleman who guards my every movement. That's enough of me. How are you? How's the "Home"? How's Anton?'

'Fine. Flourishing. Improving.' There was a laugh in Sheila's voice, and then I released her hand suddenly, realising that I had been holding it for too long. 'Anton's well enough to send a message.'

'What is it?'

'Stop being an ostrich!' said Sheila.

I was puzzled for a moment, then remembered. I knew that he had been right and that I was in love, and for the time being nothing else really counted.

For perhaps twenty minutes we talked much as we had done at St. Clare. Then Cris and Clyde came in, and a servant announced dinner.

It was one of those few evenings when there was no air-raid warning in London, and there was nothing to stop us from celebrating the occasion thoroughly. Sheila did not know just what was happening, of course, but I gathered that she knew it was a send-off party. There was gaiety that night, and not the brittle kind to which I had grown so used.

Towards ten o'clock, Sheila said: 'I must be going, or Mother will be in a panic again.' She was looking at me. 'Ned, take care of yourself, and all the luck in the world.'

'That's good enough for a toast,' said Clyde.

'I've a better!' cried Cris. They were all looking at

me, and I felt a moment of embarrassment; but it was good to be among my friends, to know that whatever they said was sincere. 'To Ned,' Cris cried, 'and the great adventure!'

There was no opportunity for an anticlimax, for Sheila's coat was brought in, and in five minutes she was on the way to the London office of the 'Home'. I went with her, but it was all too short a walk.

We stopped on the porch of the house, and I took Sheila's key from her bag, and opened the door.

'God keep you,' she said.

I gripped her shoulders, and then I kissed her. It was a long kiss and my whole heart was in it.

I stood her aside, and turned away; nor did I look back. When I was ten yards along the road I heard the door close sharply, and for the first time I wondered whether I had been wrong to leave her without a word.

I don't think so. Remember where I was going, and what I had to expect; only a fool refuses to anticipate the worst in certain circumstances, for only by doing so is there a real chance of averting it. I could not say with any certainty that I would ever see her again; that being so I would have been unjustified in attempting to tie her down to someone who might so easily become but a memory.

In Clyde's house, Cris and Clyde were still talking.

'You've time for one more drink,' Cris said, 'and then to bed. We're leaving here at four.'

'Are there any more surprises waiting?' I asked.

'You know all there is to know,' Clyde assured me. 'We didn't tell you until today, Ned, in case . . .'

'In case they managed to grab me, and I was persuaded to talk,' I finished calmly. 'All right, I'm not offended.'

'Your first broadcast to the French from France is

here,' said Clyde, handing me a sealed envelope. 'You'll get one of these every other day. Amend and alter with anything you learn over there, but I needn't tell you about that part of the job!'

Half an hour later I was in bed and asleep.

Cris called me just before four o'clock.

There is no need for me to describe at any great length the journey first to a London aerodrome, and then to Cris's base. Very little time was lost, and the moon was still shining as we took off from that ghostly aerodrome in Kent, the nose of the aircraft pointing towards the Channel.

'*To Ned, and the great adventure,*' Cris had said.

In that brief hour of flight I felt exalted, as if it were indeed a great adventure. The quiet contentment I experienced was not broken until the Channel was out of sight behind us, and the moon had gone, leaving only the stars. Once or twice in the distance we saw the landing lights of aircraft, and in the greater distance was the red glow of a fire.

Then, abruptly and without warning, the quiet disappeared.

I saw a series of what looked like phosphorescent streaks coming towards us, while at the same moment Cris at the controls exclaimed aloud. As our plane began to climb sharply, the bullets from the German nightfighter went under us. We twisted and turned for five nerve-racking minutes, my heart racing with fright.

Finally the firing lessened, then ceased altogether.

I looked down.

We were passing over a town of some size. Searchlights began to carve their way through the air, straight and deadly as some geometrical octopus. Once the nose of the plane was caught, and it seemed to me as if the whole of France woke up to throw explosives at us. But the range was bad, and we were never in greater danger than with the first shot, although once or twice shrapnel rattled against the fuselage and the wings.

The night fell quiet soon after that, and we flew for half an hour without any suggestion of interruption. I knew that we were going to land between Rouen and Louviers, but had no idea that we had flown almost due south from the last town where the ack-ack had snarled at us, then east, then nearly due north. The roar of the engine was the only sound, and then I heard Cris call out something.

A moment later a profound silence filled the cabin.

It startled me so much that I jumped in my seat, not realising at first that he had cut out the engine. Through my window, as we glided down, I saw a light flash: green, red, white.

Cris's voice sounded loud in the uncanny silence.

'We won't be long now, Ned.'

'You can't land without the engine,' I protested.

'We can in this little number,' said Cris with a laugh in his voice. 'That's what it's made for.'

I had not realised until then that it was possible to make a good and safe landing without the engine with any degree of certainty; I suppose the certainty depends on the ability of the pilot. At all events we went down like a great silent bird, until the wheels bumped against earth. We taxied along in the darkness for what seemed an incredible time, and once the plane lurched sickeningly to one side, but at last Cris pulled at the brakes and we stopped.

'One radio star, safely delivered,' said Cris, turning in his seat. 'We're handing you over to Hewison here, Ned, and taking two people back with us.'

I climbed stiffly from my seat. Half a dozen shadowy figures were standing about. Two of them exchanged a few gruff words with Cris, and then they took my place.

Cris was speaking to one of the largest of the remaining figures.

'Here he is, Hewey. Look after him. I'll be seeing you the night after tomorrow, Ned.'

We shook hands, and he went back to the plane. Before it started off, and the silence was shattered by the roar of its engine, the man named Hewison had taken my arm and was ushering me away from the spot, into my future.

13

I Become a Badly Wanted Man

Danger rarely becomes acute when you are prepared for it; or, as the humbler philosophers have it, the worst rarely happens. I expected to be on the run almost from the moment that I landed in France; instead, I was much safer there for the first six weeks than I had been in England. I moved from one well-fitted underground transmitting station to another, each with an innocent-seeming cottage above. The families living in them were alike in two respects: they hated the Nazis, and they had sons who were prisoners of war in Germany.

Their hatred, like Cris's, was the guiding factor in their lives. They had been chosen with great care, all knew the risks and accepted them willingly. But in the many different places where I stayed, going out only after dark to stretch my legs, there was no alarm for me, at first. I was constantly amazed by the number of different stations prepared Despite my knowledge of the number of agents we had there, and the large percentage of the population with us, I had never realised that in spite of all the atrocities, the slavery which prevailed, the shortage of food which was acute, and the many other difficulties, *the French still owned France*.

The explanation of that is simple enough; the German troops of occupation could never have numbered more than a million, and while a million armed men can police a country pretty effectively, it has to be remembered that in some districts the Germans were heavily outnumbered, while in others they were concentrated to fend off the attack which, I believe, they expected to be launched from England.

It was quite possible to live for weeks in parts of France without seeing a German, but it was impossible not to feel their influence. The farms were ravaged pitilessly, causing the underground hatred to smoulder with intensity and bitterness. That, I think, is why I was able to broadcast with comparative immunity for six weeks.

I came to know several of the men at the various stations, but the one with whom I worked most, and whom I came to respect nearly as much as Clyde, was Hewison, the man who had first received me.

There was a touch of the Gaul in his dark and rather sallow face, and I fancy that his forbears must at some time have sprung from France. I liked him, and was filled with admiration at the enthusiasm with which he carried out his work.

He knew something of everything, the engineering and

technical side as much as the broadcasting and news-preparation, and the respect he earned from everyone who worked with him made it obvious that he had a real grasp of everything we touched.

Each of the stations was divided into three parts. An operational room, a dormitory or rest-room with bunks for sleeping, and a listening-room.

I do not know how many messages were brought to us, but no day passed when Hewison failed to arrive with a dozen or so letters, reading them through before he and I started to prepare the 'internal' broadcast.

It was rather less than a week before I realised first-hand that Bannister, Clyde and Cris had said nothing but the truth. The Voice was one of the most-loved things by the French, and the most hated by the Germans.

Standing out most clearly in my memory is a night early in February, when I left the station after the broadcast and went to stroll along the village street. I was in Thimert, near Chartres, a village I had not then seen by day. There was a little estaminet standing on its own some hundred yards from my cottage, and as the door opened I heard someone say:

'Tonight it was superb, Pierre, superb! And think, my friend! Three railway crashes, *three*, in one day!'

I started, for I had just told France of the three crashes, all engineered in Alsace the day before.

'Be quiet, Jacques, you will be heard,' an agitated voice muttered.

'Not here, not in little Thimert,' said Jacques with a confidence doubless fostered by his drinking. 'We are quite safe here, if there was an accursed *provocateur* I would strangle him with these two hands. Each night I speak to the good God, Pierre, each night I give thanks for the man who gives us our news, for the Englishman

104

who lives in France under the noses of the swine.'

Pierre was more cautious.

'He is good, Jacques, but—hist! I hear a movement.'

'You have the jumps, my friend, it is nothing but *la pauvre* Yvonne, watching for her man. Each night she watches for him, but he will never come.' There was bitterness in the man's voice.

Actually I had made the movement, and as I had no wish to be taken for a *provocateur* and had a considerable respect for the probable strength of that man's hands, I did not follow them. So their voices faded, but there was a warm feeling within me.

There were plenty of other indications, but I realised the real concern with which the German authorities viewed me when Hewison brought me in an envelope one day.

I opened it to find an Order of the Day issued by General von Kleister, then in control of part of the Seine province. I will translate into colloquial English:

Every effort must be made to discover and to apprehend the English broadcaster, known as the Voice, actually Norman Deane, late of the British Foreign Service.

Description: Five feet ten. Grey eyes. Square cleft chin. Small mole on the corner of right lip.

They were wrong there, the mole had been removed in London before I re-entered France.

Broad. Lean.

Any German or any French citizen proved to have listened to the Voice without orders is liable to summary punishment—in the case of the French, to be shot.

A reward of 50,000 reichmarks will be paid to the

soldier, or man or woman who gives information leading to the detention of the Voice.

I was re-reading it for the second time when Hewison came in. I handed it to him and watched him as he read.

'Do you think you should go out, even at night?' he asked at last.

'Certainly I do,' I replied promptly, for I was beginning to feel the effect of living too much under electric light. 'I'll be safe enough by night.'

'I'm not sure it's wise.'

'Perhaps not, but the alternative is less so,' I said obstinately. I had my way, but Hewison remained worried and apprehensive.

After six weeks we returned to Thimert of pleasant memory. It was nearing the middle of March, then, and the days were lengthening. It would soon be impossible for me to go out after dark unless I were to miss my sleep, which was becoming a vital factor. I was tired most of the time, and growing irritable with it. Hewison, who went out frequently, bore with me patiently and did everything he could to relieve me of the irksome boredom and loneliness.

Towards four o'clock one afternoon I was drowsing in front of an electric fire when I heard the bell which told me that Hewison or one of the others was returning through the cottage. I looked towards the door.

Hewison came in hurriedly, and before the door had properly closed snapped out:

'Get your coat on, Deane.'

'Coat?' Remember I had not been out except after dark for six weeks. 'Why, what . . . ?'

'They'll be here in twenty minutes,' Hewison grunted, stepping swiftly to the listening-room to warn the other man who was there. 'There's a car waiting at the other end of the village. I'm not coming with you, you can trust the driver.'

I was struggling into my coat by then.

Each day I had religiously packed my bag in case of an alarm. Here was the alarm, and I was not caught so unprepared as I might have been.

It was a cold but clear day. The bright light hurt my eyes as I groped in my pocket for smoked glasses.

'Hurry, *M'sieu*,' an old man's voice urged me. '*Nom d'un nom*, they will be here!'

It was the old peasant whom I had met several times, and when he realised that I was temporarily blinded he gripped my elbow and hurried me on.

'To your right, *M'sieu*, the car. May the good God look after you.'

I hurried to the right, where a car was standing outside the estaminet; then drew up sharply, for the man at the wheel wore the Gestapo uniform.

For a moment I was panicked, believing that I was too late.

A French voice said crisply: 'Get in, please, there is no time to lose.'

It was a big Mercedes Benz, glistening with chromium fittings, a luxury car of the kind often seen when Hitler drove through the streets of Berlin. I climbed in the back and before I had closed the door the driver was letting in the clutch and we were away.

The car roared out of the straggling village. It would not be long before dusk came, and with it the darkness which, for my part, I wanted more than anything else. I had learned enough of running from the Nazis to be sure that only by night was it even reasonably safe.

The road was bad. Pot-holes jerked the Benz so

severely that I grabbed at the strap to keep myself from lurching forward against the front seats. The driver drove with the highly developed recklessness which is singular to the French; in fact his driving reassured me more than anything else. No German would ever drive with such a disregard for printed signs.

At least, I thought, the driver knew what he was doing and where he was going; that gave him an advantage over me, but also relieved me of the need of worrying. When Thimert was five or six miles behind us, and we were going over flat, uninteresting country, I settled back as comfortably as the road would permit.

But it was not long before we were running into the outskirts of Chartres, going over cobbled roads at far too fierce a pace. There were bicycles by the hundred in the town, and the pavements were thronged, but we passed no other private car.

Now we were weaving in and out of cyclists and pedestrians with no regard for the safety of men or women.

As we continued onward there was a roar coming from a hundred throats, and a dozen women appeared in the road in front of us, fists clenched and shaken in violent anger. Missiles began to strike the side of the car. Something squashed against the window near me. Once I thought I saw the gleam of a knife.

There was danger in that crowd, a menace which made me understand something of the perils of a German's life in occupied France. I even wondered whether we would be dragged from the car, but three or four *gendarmes* appeared, waving their white batons and shouting and gesticulating. They had revolvers, too. The threat was sufficient to make the crowd disperse.

The driver bellowed at the *gendarmes* with a fluency

in bastard French which had to be heard to be believed. He drove on.

It seemed to me that the news of the incident had spread throughout Chartres. I have never known a more nerve-racking drive. My fears of capture and the alarm at Thimert faded completely in the dangers of deliberate obstruction that beset us.

At last we reached the open road again.

We drove on at speed but I was finished with silence, and tapped the driver on the shoulder. He looked round and grinned. Something in that grin was vaguely familiar, but it was not until a little later that I realised that; for the moment I was too incensed. I tapped his shoulder again, and bellowed:

'Stop, stop immediately!'

I thought he was going to defy me. Instead he pulled into the side of the road and looked round again, no longer smiling but sober-faced.

'You need to stop, *M'sieu*?'

'I'm coming in front with you,' I said. 'What the devil d'you mean by creating those scenes in Chartres? Have you gone mad?'

'No more mad than is necessary to act the part of a German,' said the driver. 'With the whole district alarmed and looking for you, how else would we have got through? No one was hurt, I made sure of that.'

'You could have avoided Chartres,' I told him as I climbed into the seat next to him. 'What sense was there in going through the town at all?'

'It was the only road not covered by the Gestapo,' said the driver simply. He looked at me with a devil-may-care grin that not only reminded me of that first hint of recognition, but told me who it was.

Anton Duval! I could hardly believe it.

'Anton!' I exclaimed. 'Anton, you . . .'

'Just wait until it is dark and we are off the road,' said Anton, 'and you may talk as much as you like, Ned. Meanwhile—on we go!' He put the car forward at a speed which made talk impossible.

I was so flabbergasted that I said nothing, but obeyed his unspoken command to sit back and keep quiet. I think I would have stayed in a dazed, half-somnambulant condition but for the armed men who suddenly sprang across the road, and the barrier of wood and poles which lay beyond.

14

I First Hear of the Liberator

Anton trod sharply on the brakes, and the men immediately opened the doors. They were husky fellows, and their guns looked ugly.

A hand gripped my shoulder, and another gripped Anton's.

He spoke swiftly, in French.

'That is quite enough!' The words would serve little purpose, I thought, and was prepared to be dragged into the road. Nevertheless, the grip loosened on my shoulder. There was a short, tense pause.

'*There cannot be enough until we have reached the end of the road.*'

'*It is not as far as you think,*' said Anton.

The man released me, then, and a startling change came over the faces of the party, five in all. There was a note of excitement in their voices, and they began to speak at once. I was so bewildered that only one word impressed iteslf in my mind: '*Liberateur*'.

The Liberator, I thought. What are they talking about?

Finally, careful directions were given. Turn right, left, right again. So often did we have to turn, in fact, that I doubted whether Anton would remember enough to find the way to our rendezvous. At last, with a hail of *bon voyages*, the men backed from the car.

'*Vive le Liberateur!*' the director cried.

It was taken up by the others, the cry, thin and ghostly, following us as we sped on our way.

By then the darkness was falling so fast that I could barely see Anton's face. He seemed to be smiling to himself, however. I felt a surge of annoyance. It did not matter where we were or what we did, there always seemed to be a conspiracy, a mystery from which I was excluded.

'Anton,' I said firmly, 'I'm not going to stand this any longer. Who are they? What is this talk about the Liberator?'

'You'll hear plenty of him soon enough, Ned. Meanwhile our anxiety is to get away safely. Some swine betrayed you at Thimert, and I only heard of it at the last moment. Had you been caught I could not have faced Cris again.'

'Are we going to another station?' I asked.

'No,' said Anton quietly. 'We cannot reach one tonight. There is a little place in the forest further along where we can stay for the night. Cris will be there, or will arrive in the next few hours.'

I had to be satisfied with that. Anton was too intent on

driving and finding his way to talk, and I had the sense not to try to make him.

I was thinking of his recovery, of Sheila, and a dozen other things but in my mind the obsession was '*le Liberateur*'. There was a romantic ring about the name. '*Vive le Liberateur!*' There had been real feeling in that cry.

After perhaps an hour, we turned off the main road. Trees reared up beside us. After a few seconds Anton switched off the headlamps, and went along slowly, only the side-lights revealing the way.

It was one of the most uncomfortable rides I have ever taken. The road earlier had been bad enough, but this was the most baleful kind of cart-track. We lurched from side to side, and frequently I heard the wings scraping against low-lying branches.

Suddenly Anton exclaimed: '*Bien, nous voici!*'

About us was a darkness relieved only by a faint glow ahead—a phosphorescence shaped in the form of an 'L'.

'How do you know?' I demanded.

'The sign of the Liberator,' Anton said simply.

We climbed out. The sign had disappeared by then, and we stood in utter darkness. It was uncanny, and my nerves were not in the best of condition. I was apt to forget that I had been virtually imprisoned for six weeks. I stood quite still, hearing a rustling nearby; it grew gradually louder.

Then a familiar voice said: 'All safe, Anton?'

'Cris!' I exclaimed.

I saw only a vague shape, but our hands gripped and my pressure was vigorous.

'Hallo, Ned. I was afraid we might be going to lose you.'

'Damn you!' I said. 'Do you know everything?'

'I wish I did.' He took my arm, and led the way down some kind of path, Anton close behind us. After five minutes' walking, the shape of a cottage loomed up. 'A charcoal-burner's hut, Ned. It smells, but you'll get used to that.'

It did indeed, and I only hoped he was right. But it was warm in the small, stone-paved room, and there was an oil stove burning. Cris poured me out a mug of coffee.

'Are we alone here?' I asked as I drank it.

'Just the three of us for the moment. Others may turn up later. Did you have much trouble?'

'None, excepting a hold-up by a bunch of toughs who seemed to go crazy at the word "*liberateur*",' I said scathingly, 'and discounting the fact that Anton drove through Chartres like seven devils trying to impress Goering.'

'You were lucky,' Cris said soberly. 'Hewison had to blow the place up ten minutes after you'd gone; the Gestapo were on to it all right. They've found four of the other places, too. We thought we were sitting pretty, but they've been waiting to pounce. They started for the five stations at once, all of them in this area. You'll be off the air for a few days, Ned.'

'What?' I said. The statement hit me like a physical blow.

'It can't be helped,' Cris told me. 'The nearest station is a hundred miles from here, and you can't possibly get to it in time. I don't think you need worry too much, though.' He looked at his wrist-watch, then bent over a receiving set. There was an immediate crackling, and then the opening notes of Beethoven's Fifth Symphony, which always preceded my broadcast.

As the notes died away I sat quite rigid in my chair. *For my own voice appeared to be speaking.*

This is the voice of England, calling to the French from France.

A pause, and then the first verse of the French National Anthem, a rustle of papers, and:

Good evening, people of France. You will like to know, first, that Hitler and those who work with him have received yet another shock on hearing this; they imagined that they had closed down this transmitting station, but they make the mistake of thinking that it is possible to silence the voice of the Englishman uttering the spirit of France. They can hunt where they will, but they will never find the Voice, nor will they prevent it talking to you night after night until the need is gone, and the Tricolour flies proudly over Paris again. Who knows whether the date for that is not nearer than we can hope, nearer even than Hitler fears?
You have heard . .

'Cris,' I cried, 'what does this mean?'

He stretched out a hand and switched off the radio. There was a moment of eerie silence before he answered:

'We've had to prepare against emergency, Ned, you'll know that. Your impersonator—remember the man in London?—is talking for you. And there are two or three others. Whatever happens, the Voice will go on.'

I hardly knew whether to be relieved or disgruntled. Gradually I had come to look on *my* voice as the thing that mattered, and I suppose it would not have been human not to have felt a momentary twinge of disappointment. It went quickly enough, for I realised the importance of what he had told me.

'I couldn't expect to go on forever,' I said. 'That man's got me to a T.'

'He looks like you, too,' said Cris, 'and he's the model for several others. Ned, I've a note from Clyde for you.'

I opened it, disappointed that it was not from Sheila. In the poor light I smoothed out the paper, and read:

Dear Ned,

You'll get this only when you've been driven out of one of the stations and can't return easily. Cris will have told you by the time you read it that we have perfected a system by which the Voice can be carried on.

I think you should have this opportunity of coming back to England. On the other hand there will be plenty for you to do in France from time to time, not only with broadcasting. Cris will give you other details.

Whatever you decide will be perfectly all right with me. In any case I hope to see you before long.

Sincerely,
Alan Clyde

I refolded the paper carefully, and put it in my coat pocket.

'I hardly expected this kind of attitude after one alarm, Cris. Is it necessary?'

'You've been living under a strain long enough,' said Cris. 'You couldn't keep it up indefinitely, as you've already admitted. There's no need for it, anyhow. The Voice is going well, and you're free to do as you like. There's plenty to be done in England,' he added.

I said carefully: 'What does he mean by "not only with broadcasting"?'

'He means that you can help me here.'

'But aren't you on the ferry-service?'

'From time to time, yes,' said Cris, 'but things keep moving into different channels; we can't make set plans for long. It's becoming increasingly obvious that a newer and stronger organisation has to be built up over here. We've pilots in plenty to take people to England, but it's getting damned hard to get them out of Nazi hands. Too many of them have been caught lately, and there's a leakage of information.' He paused, while I considered the importance of what he told me. 'We make arrangements to have so-and-so ready,' Cris went on slowly, 'and so-and-so either gets shot or taken to Germany. We're not sure who's doing it, but we are sure that it's no longer wise to make any of our arrangements known through our usual channels.'

'Clarify that,' I said quietly.

'*Le voilà!*' exclaimed Anton. 'Never have I heard such a man! Here is two, and here is another two. Add them together for me, please! Ned, you were in the British Diplomatic Service too long!'

'Just as well to have everything in duplicate,' said Cris with a grin. 'Now listen, Ned. We've worked with an organisation consisting of French and English agents. They've contrived until now to get men who have wanted to leave France ready for us, and we've picked them up as we did when you arrived in France. It worked smoothly until a fortnight ago, when our men began to fail to turn up. We've lost two planes, too, and the pilots. The landing-ground was surrounded when the boys arrived, and they didn't have a chance. We've other landing-grounds,' he added, 'but we've got to narrow down the scope. If we want a man we've got to get him ourselves, and there's to be no general announcement even amongst our friends. Got it?'

'How can I help?' I demanded.

'You speak French like a native, and German so well that you'd pass for one if you put your mind to it,' said Cris. 'There's a vacancy for a man who'll join Anton and me in getting our men safely to the landing-grounds and seeing them off. What do you think of it?'

'It's all right if it will work,' I said cautiously. 'But surely it would be better to stop the leakage?'

'That's not our job,' said Cris. 'There are plenty of Secret Intelligence men doing that, or trying to. We can't hold up the ferry-service until the leakage is stopped.'

Anton exploded.

'*Mon Dieu* Ned! Must you look this way and that before you say "Yes"! I have never heard so much talk!'

I glared at him across the dimly lit room.

'One day you might learn the wisdom of doing just that,' I said tartly. 'You wouldn't have been knocked out if you'd stopped to think before running after Garat.'

'*Touché*,' said Anton good-humouredly. 'But, Ned, listen to me . . .'

I was slowly beginning to feel the fascination of what they proposed.

'How long have you been working on your own?'

'Just over a month,' said Cris.

'And they've dubbed him *le Liberateur*!' exclaimed Anton. 'Five times in the past month, Ned, he has lifted victims from beneath the noses of the Nazis. There are a hundred thousand who will help us in occupied France, a million in the unoccupied districts. France is hungry for hope and receptive to it. First the Voice, and now *le Liberateur!* It has romance, as I have told you, and the French will always react to that. I know my people!'

Anton was more enthusiastic than I can ever remember him, and his eyes were flashing even in that poor light. 'It is a magnificent conception, a new Pimpernel . . .'

'The Baroness Orczy would be delighted,' I said drily. 'You can count me in, Cris, of course.'

Cris chuckled.

' "Of course" is right. After you've had a sleep I've a job for you.'

'Oh,' I said, and then laughed. 'Drat you, I certainly can't call my life my own! But . . .' I paused, and then went on sharply: 'Surely I'm too well known in France? My description must be on record.' Another thought struck me. 'Your disguise isn't permanent, Anton, is it? Your eyes . . .'

'An hour, and I can be myself again,' said Anton. 'Don't worry. I wonder . . . ?'

He stopped abruptly.

While he was talking I saw Cris move slowly towards the door. Now I saw that he had his right hand in his pocket, and his left was held towards Anton, exhorting silence. Anton rose to his feet. The only sound then was our breathing, except the thumping of my heart, which would not stop but seemed to me to echo in every corner of the room.

Then I heard footsteps.

They were slow and hesitant. I watched the door, fascinated, while Cris's hand came out of his pocket holding an automatic.

There was a faint tap on the door.

Slowly, slowly, it began to open.

15

The Case of M'sieu le Grisson

I have tried to relate the incidents of this part of my life clearly and dispassionately while endeavouring at the same time to record my own reaction to them. At the start I said that it was primarily a story of Crispian St. Clare; to me, Cris will always be the central figure. Yet it was not until that evening that I came face to face with something of what he was actually doing and for me the great adventure really started. The rest, the earlier part, was essential to it, of course, the later idea evolving gradually, altered by whatever emergency or tactics demanded. I suppose it was inevitable that sooner or later things had to go wrong with our widespread organisation in France so that some details, particularly the smuggling of important personalities out of France, had to be left to a smaller faction of English or pro-English men.

None of those things entered my mind as I watched the door slowly opening. Cris stood quite still, a little behind it. Anton covered the door, while I had visions of a tommy-gun and a horde of jack-booted Gestapo agents forcing their way through.

For this I sat waiting, my teeth clenched.

Suddenly Anton said: '*Ça va bien*, Cris.'

He pulled the door more widely open, and a girl stepped through.

Why I was so surprised I hardly know, but my world had been entirely made up of men for a long time, and I had expected a man. Instead, it was a girl. She entered swiftly, and Cris closed the door behind her.

She wore a shawl over her head so that little of her face was visible. When she moved the shawl back it was seen to be a pure oval; pale and piquant, her eyes enormous.

She stared at Cris, and then said quietly: '*M'sieu le Liberateur*?' The words sounded very strange and matter-of-fact. I remember that I was startled, even appalled, that she should know Cris by his soubriquet, although second thoughts told me that she had merely guessed at it, knowing that the *Liberateur* would be in the charcoal-burner's hut, but not knowing which of the three of us he was.

'I can take him a message, *Mam'selle*,' said Cris quietly.

The situation remained a little uncanny, not less so because the girl's voice was low-pitched, not in any way alarmed, and very pure. It was easy to see that here was no village girl but an educated Frenchwoman.

'Then tell him,' she said, 'that M'sieu le Grisson will be ready tomorrow night.'

'Is he well?'

'As well as one can expect, yes.' The girl hesitated, then spoke in a more tense voice and with a passion which startled me. '*M'sieu*, will you get him away safely?'

'Yes,' promised Cris.

'The good God will thank you.' As she turned away Cris put out a hand and touched her shoulder.

'Who knows that you left the house?' he asked.

'No one, *M'sieu*.'

'Are you sure?'

'As sure as it is possible for me to be.'

Cris looked across at Anton.

'Will you see her back, Anton?'

Anton said that he would, so quickly that I was surprised; I did not know that he was so impressionable, and had been foolish enough to imagine that to him Sheila was as all-important as she was to me. A moment later Cris and I were alone.

'By George, that scared me,' I said. 'Cris, I don't like taking this "Why? Why?" angle all the time, but is it necessary to mystify me with everything that happens?'

Cris shrugged. 'It's not necessary, Ned, it just happens. I expected a message from le Grisson, but I'd no idea how it would come or who would bring it. He told me he would get word to me, that's all.'

'Who is le Grisson?'

'A big landowner about here who has been working against the Nazis for some time. It's getting too dangerous for him. Vichy has sent several inspectors to ask him questions, and it won't be long before they discover what he's been doing. We've to get him out before they do. It's not easy, he's been ill for some weeks. That's why the trouble started; he left his affairs to a manager he thought he could trust.'

'What kind of affairs?' I demanded.

'Every kind of nuisance for Vichy and Berlin,' said Cris. 'Sabotage, attacks on Gestapo agents, the kind of stuff you've been putting out night after night. Le Grisson's organised what amounts to a guerilla band, several hundred strong. They prowl by night, taking stores earmarked for the Hun, and they're dangerous customers to Vichy. You met some of them on the road. The guerillas need arms, and le Grisson gets them distributed. We bring them over.'

He told me as simply as that, yet there remained a question in my mind, although I was determined not to utter it.

'What's the question, Ned?'

'Oh, it doesn't matter. I'm beginning to agree with Anton, I can't add two and two together.'

'Don't be an ass. What's on your mind?'

'Well,' I said, 'le Grisson's probably done a lot of good here, but . . .' I hesitated, and then blurted out: 'Aren't there more important people to get to England? Does he count for anything outside this little part of France? Won't he be taking up room that should be kept for someone else?'

Cris began to take some tins out of the cupboard, while I picked up a bread-knife and began slicing a loaf.

'Up to a point you're right,' he said. 'But consider the value of it in the long run. Here's a man Vichy's after. They prepare to pounce, and lo! he's not there. It's going to get on their nerves, Ned.'

'I suppose so,' I said. I sat down heavily, the food in front of me suddenly tasteless and unappetising. 'I don't want anything to eat. I feel tired out, blast it.'

'Nothing to blast about,' said Cris. 'You've been burrowing underground too long. You'd better have a snack, though, and then get to bed.'

I did as he said, and once in my bunk I fell fast asleep.

I awakened without a headache for the first time for a month.

After a few minutes I climbed slowly out of my bunk, and saw that Anton was sleeping in the one above me. I put on my shoes and coat—I had kept my other clothes on—and looked about for some water. There was none in the hut, but when I reached the door and opened it I saw Cris stripped to the waist dousing his body from a tin bowl.

'He looked up.

' 'Morning, Ned. How do you feel?'

'I'm fine,' I said, 'and I'll be better for a wash.' I stifled a yawn and looked about me.

The clearing was so small that it scarcely deserved the name. Beyond the hut were trees, nothing but trees.

I flung a half-bucket of water over myself, and felt the better for it. Breakfast was out of a tin except for the bread and coffee.

'Cris,' I said, dismissing as ignoble all thoughts of bacon and eggs, 'I've been thinking about that girl. Why did le Grisson send her?'

'A girl slipping out of a house after dark arouses less comment than a man. Le Grisson's afraid that the house is watched.'

'Who is she?'

'She works in le Grisson's kitchen,' Cris told me. 'She was one of the richest heiresses in France, until the German occupation. She lost everything, her people, her money, and her friends. He heard of her and gave her employment, which was an excuse to give her food and clothes. He's done more than anyone I know, so far, to try and help the people who have suffered most. The trouble is that there are so many, and no individual can cater for the masses. Yvonne is comparatively lucky.' He laughed harshly. 'That's France, today. My God, it sickens me!' He was so rarely demonstrative that I was startled out of an uneasy contemplation of what he had been saying.

'When you get a man like le Grisson, who will fight and keep fighting for what little decency he can retrieve for others as well as himself,' Cris went on, 'it's rare and refreshing, Ned. But this is just wasting time!' He looked at me speculatively, before continuing: 'We've got to do something about that face of yours. You haven't shaved—all the better. Your hair's fairly long . . .' He pursed his lips. 'We can narrow your eyes, and fill up the cleft in your chin. That should do it.'

'Who's the plastic surgeon?' I demanded.

'I am,' said Cris. 'Paraffin wax and a hypo is all we need for the cleft, and some gum for the eyes. It isn't painful.'

The whole operation, if that is what it can be called, took a little under half an hour. It was not painful, as Cris had said, but far from comfortable.

'You'll get used to it,' he told me. 'It took Anton a couple of days, no more'

As he spoke Anton himself appeared.

'Ah, a man of parts. Perhaps even an improvement. How many questions has he been asking this morning? Last night I counted one hundred and three.'

'Anton,' I said, half-amused, but only half, 'something happened to you when you were at St. Clare. The blow on the head must have caused it. You were always high-spirited, but now you're unbearable. What makes you so pleased with life?'

'My work!' declared Anton, flourishing a fork. 'I am first assistant to the Liberator. That is something to be proud of, my friend. Even you, apprentice as you are, should feel so. *Eh, mon Cris?*'

Cris was bending over a bundle, pulling out some clothes.

'Put these on, Ned,' he said, 'and let the idiot burble on.'

I donned the garments Cris produced, which, though ragged, were clean enough. I wondered when I should wear my own suit again, for the future seemed vague and uncertain. He proceeded to explain some of the things which puzzled me. As peasants, we were to be members of the guerilla band which le Grisson had organised; he, Cris, had already captured their imagination, and arrangements had been made for him to lead them when le Grisson left the country. Clear-cut plans, at the moment, were non-existent; but messages would reach us from England from time to time, and when any man was named we were to get him.

'Supposing you tell me what my job is for this morning?' I suggested, stepping to the window where there was a small mirror, and examining myself critically.

It was not a pretty sight. My already plain face was now positively villainous; I decided gloomily that there were many criminals who looked less debased than I did then.

'You're going up to the house,' said Cris. 'Le Grisson has some information he wants to leave with us, and doesn't speak English.'

Secretly I thought that there was no reason why I should have been disguised for that task, but I made no comment. Anton was left at the hut, and with Cris I went into the forest.

The undergrowth was thick, but there was a well-defined track leading through it, beneath the bare branches of the trees. Dead leaves softened our tread.

Suddenly Cris stopped.

I should have said before that, except that he had not shaved, he looked very much as he had always done, and his fair stubble did not make him look so disreputable as mine. He walked as always with his head well back, and with a peculiar lightness of tread.

'What . . . ?' I began.

He pressed my arm.

Again I heard the sound of approach much later than he did. It appeared to be coming from our right. I peered through the trees, while Cris kept quite still.

Slowly a figure appeared. It was an old man who was limping, one foot slurring more than the other.

'Jules, my friend,' Cris called softly.

The old man swung round. The expression in his eyes was strange, to me; obviously he regarded Cris with a deep regard, even awe; but also he was frightened. He could not speak without taking in a great gulp of air, and I found it difficult at first to understand him.

Then: 'It is too late, *M'sieu*, they have got him.'

Cris said levelly: 'Are you sure?'

'Not twenty minutes ago they called,' said the old man. 'Already they are making him dress. It is too late, *M'sieu*.' He kept staring at Cris as if expecting an oracle to speak; and the oracle did, for Cris said sharply:

'Go on to the hut, Jules, and warn Anton to be ready for an immediate start.'

'Yes, *M'sieu*, yes!' A light sprang into Jules's eyes and he turned and limped away, while I stared at Cris as he gripped my shoulder and urged me forward.

'You're in the thick of it quicker than I expected,' he said. 'We'll have trouble getting le Grisson out now.' He took his right hand from his pocket and pushed an automatic into mine. 'You might need that. I've another.'

He set a cracking pace for five minutes, and I found it difficult to keep up with him: evidence that my unhealthy life for the past six weeks had softened me, for normally Cris cannot outwalk me; it is one of the few things I can do better than he. I set my lips and made myself keep up, until suddenly we reached the end of the trees and saw before us a stretch of meadowland.

Beyond was the house Cris had talked of.

It was a square building, pleasant, but not particularly impressive.

Outside the front door were two cars.

'That'll mean eight or nine men,' I said pessimistically.

'Perhaps,' said Cris. He did not seem in any way perturbed, but walked across the meadow in full view of the house. My instinctive thought was to find cover of some kind, but I realised then that it was not necessary, for either of us could have been natives of the district and there was nothing particularly suspicious about our appearance.

A *gendarme* was sitting on the running-board of one of the cars. By him was a carbine rifle, so ancient that it made me smile. He was an oldish man, frowning ferociously at us, and my façade of self-assurance began to fade. He grabbed the carbine and stepped in our path.

'No one is to enter,' he growled.

'No one?' asked Cris, and to my astonishment added: 'Not even the Liberator, my friend?' He spoke very quietly while eyeing the man, whose mouth dropped open. The carbine almost fell from his grasp as he breathed:

'*Le Liberateur!*'

'Is Laval to take le Grisson?' Cris asked quietly.

'You entered by the back way, *M'sieu*,' the *gendarme* said in a hoarse voice. '*Je n'ai vu personne, M'sieu.*' His eyes shifted away from us as we walked past him to the front door.

It was standing ajar.

I had never dreamed that the approach would be so direct, or that the effect of that soubriquet would be so great; against it that of the Voice positively paled. But I had no time to wonder, for as we stepped into the hall the girl who had brought us the message the night before appeared, her piquant face set and expressionless.

'They won't talk to him for long. Go into the forest,

Yvonne,' Cris said quietly. 'As far and deep into it as you can, to the hut if possible, and hurry.'

By the foot of the wide staircase Cris paused, and looked at me with a half-smile.

'We may get through without a scrap, Ned, but if we don't, hit them where it hurts most. The probability is that they're so sure of themselves they won't be expecting us. All right?'

'All right,' I assured him.

We went quietly up the stairs, and when we reached the first landing, heard French voices above us. A moment later I saw an armed man standing outside a door with a fixed bayonet. He was one of Pétain's military police, and I did not like the look of his coarse, beetle-browed face.

Cris said: 'I'll get him to turn his back to you. Keep out of sight for a moment.'

I stayed on the landing. Cris went up quietly then, but with no attempt at concealment. I was just able to see him approach the *poilu* with a finger pressed to his lips. The man was so surprised that he kept silent, and I heard a faint whisper from Cris.

'The *gendarme* outside has been attacked,' Cris said. 'If you are quiet you will be in time to surprise the attacker. If you doubt me, look through the window.' He pointed to a window, and the man turned, but was not, I realised, going to take the bait so easily. Nevertheless he turned with Cris so that his back was towards me, and I covered the next half a dozen stairs swiftly.

Cris had moved by then, poking his automatic into the man's waist; I believe he could have done as much on his own as he did with me, up to that moment at all events.

The *poilu* stiffened.

I reached him then, and wrenched his gun away, spinning him round. Cris hit him behind the ear with the butt of the automatic, caught him, and lowered him with scarcely a sound.

'He's all right for five minutes,' Cris said, 'and that's all we want. You get le Grisson away, and don't worry about me. Hurry down the drive, on foot. Anton will meet you somewhere along the right-hand road.'

He did not wait to hammer home his instructions but turned the handle of the door of the room. The voices were still coming, harshly for the most part.

Cris flung the door open, and levelled his automatic towards the men there. There were five in all. Four were middle-aged and in the uniform of the *gendarmerie*, one was very much older, grey-haired and grey-bearded.

'*M'sieu* le Grisson,' I said. 'This way, please.'

It looks absurd, written down, but I can remember very distinctly that those were the words I used.

Le Grisson moved towards me.

One of the others made as though to stop him, and I reached him in time to deliver a punch to the chin which jolted him severely, although it had nothing like the power it should have done, for I was a long way from being at my best. At all events it sent him staggering, and as he fell I snatched the revolver from his holster and stuffed it in my pocket.

Cris said: 'If another of you moves, he will be dead by morning.' He was almost nonchalant. 'The Liberator says so,' he added, and I fancied he used the name with a certain amount of satisfaction.

I was astonished at its effect, the three men who remained upright took their hands from their belts, where they had been dangerously close to their guns, and kept quite still.

I saw no purpose in leaving them their weapons, and removed them one after another. Le Grisson picked up a brief-case and went with me to the door.

He did not speak until we were in the hall.

Then: 'There will be a *gendarme* outside.'

'He has a conscience,' I said. 'He let us in.'

It satisfied the old man, who moved forward towards the half-open door.

The *gendarme*, who was sitting on the running-board with the carbine between his knees, looked up but did not move. I kept a grip on le Grisson's arm, and we hurried along the drive. I could see the road to the right, winding away into the forest in the direction opposite to that from which Cris and I had come, and along it I saw a car travelling towards us.

By the time we reached the drive gates, Anton had pulled up and was opening the back door. Le Grisson climbed in.

I felt strangely alone when he had gone, and I stood near the drive, watching the car out of sight. I was aware of a sense of deflation. While there had been the need for action I had been perfectly all right, but now I was acutely conscious of being a badly wanted man standing where anyone who wished could see me, while Cris was alone in the house with four—no, five—Vichy Frenchmen.

Very soon I knew that I was not alone; I saw men approaching the house from three directions, ignoring me as if I did not exist. Rough-clad and hard-faced, they converged on the front door as I watched them breathlessly.

16

I See Four Men of Vichy

I do not know what I expected.

I was almost sure that the men were the 'guerillas', and equally so that Anton had seen them and told them not to pay me any attention. Yet there remained a faint nagging doubt of anxiety; supposing I were wrong, and they were enemies?

I had something under three minutes in which to worry, for Cris came from the house then. They all stopped a few yards away from him, and I saw Cris smile. He said something I could not catch, then climbed into one of the cars and drove it towards me. The others went into the house. I was puzzled by the disappearance of the old *gendarme* until I saw him peering round a bush near the door, holding his carbine. Suddenly he raised it and fired three times into the air.

Cris pulled up alongside me.

'We'll watch from here,' he said. 'Easy, isn't it?'

'Yes.' It was so easy that I suspected there would be a serious snag, while I was puzzled by his 'we'll watch from here'. I suppose I had half an idea of what would develop, for already the antics of the *gendarme* had told me much. He had fired into the air to make it appear that he had tried to stop the advance of the guerillas. (The men were not actually guerillas, for many of them worked during the day, and they did not move together in a party; but the word is more apposite than 'saboteurs' and they themselves preferred it.) In spite of my close contact with

France by radio and the countless reports I had read, the first day or two of my travels told me much more than I had hitherto realised of the resurgent spirit of the people. Whoever imagines that the war in France stopped with Pétain's shameful armistice is sadly mistaken.

Cris sat back in his seat, his face calm and expressionless.

'Here they come,' he said at last.

Out from the house came, presumably, one of the Vichy officials. I should say 'presumably', for he had no uniform to distinguish him. He was mother-naked, and was propelled by one of the guerillas. I could see that he was frightened out of his wits.

Before he had reached the drive a second man appeared in a similar plight. A third and a fourth followed. I watched the men running across the rough meadowland towards the forest, their cries gradually fading.

I drew a deep breath and looked at Cris. There was a faint smile on his lips as he let in the clutch, but I doubt whether he was particularly amused. I hoped he was not.

'Anton would have enjoyed that,' he said drily.

'Won't the guerillas be recognised?' I asked.

'Probably, but they've a price on their heads already,' Cris told me. 'One more show like this won't make any difference to them, they'll be imprisoned for duration at best if they're taken. Did you hear anything about Yvonne?'

'Anton said she was on the way to the hut.'

'We'll have to move from there, I'm afraid. The forest will be combed out in the next twenty-four hours and the hut's far too conspicuous. We'll go further south,' he added.

I thought swiftly of what I knew of the country.

Once we reached the vicinity of Orléans itself, and crossed the Loire, which presumably we would do if we were going south, there was marshy land; and in March it would be at its worst. Some of the stretches of country were bogged up until the first really dry spell, and I had heard many stories of wayfarers being lost completely in the marshes, their bodies found only in the spring, when the land became comparatively dry. The locals could find their way about safely enough, but it was dangerous ground for strangers.

Cris drove steadily along the bad road into the forest. I suppose we were travelling for half an hour. Then he pulled up, the thickening trees making progress impossible. He took the distributor-head from the car, and we followed the path on foot. Another ten minutes brought us to the hut.

Yvonne must have seen us for she came hurrying out. Ignoring me completely, she demanded of Cris:

'Is he safe?'

'Perfectly safe, Yvonne.'

There followed one of the most touching moments of my life. I was the onlooker, and yet it affected me as it must have affected the main actors. Yvonne stepped forward and took his right hand, raising it slowly to her lips. Then she released it, and smiled gently into his face before turning away.

'What are you going to do now?' Cris asked her.

'I shall stay here, *M'sieu*, as I did before.'

Cris nodded, but I could almost see his mind working. He was reminding himself that whatever qualities the guerillas had, they were amongst the most uxorious of the European races. Many of them would doubtless have been without their women for months on end.

It was no place for Yvonne. I was quite sure Cris would broach the subject before the day was out.

We all entered the hut. Yvonne immediately busied herself preparing a meal.

'We're all right here for the next three or four hours,' said Cris. 'Sometime before that, one or two people I want to see will arrive. And you?'

I held up the brief-case le Grisson had given me.

'I can go through this. They'll be the records you wanted me to translate.'

Whether le Grisson had been wise or not I did not know, although I was inclined to doubt it. At all events, he had compiled a list of the sabotage done in the district, and the methods employed. The list was interesting in many ways, and I believed would ultimately be of the greatest value. It recorded the names and addresses of the Vichy supporters and Nazi collaborators. The record was written unemotionally, but I could sense the cold hatred of le Grisson, and imagine him working and conspiring to offset the plans if those he dubbed traitors.

There was one other list, of men who had left the district in an attempt to reach England, and against forty-seven of them, out of a total of a hundred and three, were little crosses in red. They indicated those who had failed.

Cris was outside when I finished a rough translation, and I went to join him. He was talking to a red-faced man with an enormous black moustache, who carried a rifle. He glanced at me inquisitively, then turned back to Cris, who was saying:

'What is Vincenne's address, Paul?'

'182, Rue de Jeanne.'

'Can you let me have two men to show me the way?'

'A dozen if *M'sieu* would like.'

'Two will be enough. How long has he been under surveillance?'

'Since yesterday midday, *M'sieu*. He is being watched by our friends also, word will come if there is any further news to report. But the danger to him, I think, is not immediate.' He paused, and then began to speak awkwardly, gathering confidence as he went on.

'Now that *M'sieu* le Grisson is gone, *M'sieu*, I am concerned for—for Yvonne.' He looked away quickly, then back to Cris. 'It is no place for her. Is it possible for her to be sent away?'

Cris said slowly: 'I've been thinking of it, Paul. What do you know of Yvonne?'

Paul smiled and held his hands apart, a gesture of wonderment mingled with respect.

'If she were a man, *M'sieu*, I would have her join us. She has done much to help, and could do more. She talks little, but she is sad. She has told me of what happened to her mother and her father, when the accursed Boche came through. She is from Alsace, you understand.'

Cris said quietly: 'I think we'll take her with us, Paul. She might be helpful. In any case we'll look after her.'

'A thousand thanks, *M'sieu*!' The words carried relief and gratitude. 'It is what I had hoped. Now, *M'sieu*, are there any more orders?'

'For the time being, no. I will send you an address soon, and you will report there of anything which needs doing hurriedly. If anyone is in danger get him away and hide him until I can send for him. And, Paul, is there a printer amongst you?'

'We can get matter printed, yes.'

Cris turned to me.

'Ned, this is more in your line than mine. What kind of a message do you think would be best?'

'For publicising the *Liberateur*?' I demanded.

'Yes. I want to keep stirring up the local officials, to keep them on edge.'

'The fewer words the better.' I took a slip of paper from the sheaf in my hand and scribbled down:

Who Saved le Grisson?
Le Liberateur

Who Will Save You and Yours?
LE LIBERATEUR!

'That ought to do for a start, anyhow,' I said.

Cris handed the paper to Paul, who read swiftly and then bent his eyes on me with approval.

'It shall be done, *M'sieu*.' He drew himself up and saluted. '*Bon voyage, M'sieu*.'

Paul went off, and Cris turned to me with a thoughtful smile.

'Who is the man Vincenne?' I asked.

'Another such as le Grisson,' said Cris, 'from Orléans. We want to get him out if we can. He's been giving us information about the production in the local factories, and passing on consignment notes so that le Grisson's men can get busy on the railway.' He chuckled again. 'You'll probably have to prove that you really can swim, and the Loire will be cold at this time of the year.'

'You're going after him?'

'Tonight, yes. I hope Anton gets back in time.'

'Where has he taken le Grisson?'

'To the other side of the forest. There's a landing-ground not far from there, and le Grisson will be able to stay until our plane arrives tonight. Ned, what do you think about the Yvonne idea?'

I hesitated before replying.

I was doubtful in some ways, and yet I believed I saw what was in his mind. Yvonne, as he had pointed out when I had first asked about her, would arouse less suspicions than a man in certain circumstances, and she would be invaluable for taking messages. That her spirit was willing I had no doubt, but there were limits to that endurance, while in an emergency I saw difficulties in which we would probably be far better off without the girl. Sentimentally I was all for it; practically I had serious doubts.

'If we take her away from here we'll have to see her through when we finish,' I said.

'When we finish there'll be no need to worry about her,' Cris said. 'We'll take her into Orléans tonight, anyhow.'

That was the first intimation I had of his astounding confidence, the confidence that he, and those with him, would see the end of a victorious war. He always took it for granted, or at least contrived to make it seem that he did. It may have been his way of making us more confident, of course.

When we returned to the hut, after two or three more of the guerillas had come, including one of the men who had raided le Grisson's house and brought with him the papers taken from the pockets of the officials, we were greeted with the appetising smell of cooking.

Yvonne was stirring a pot on the brazier, from which steam was rising.

Cris sniffed. 'Hmm. Smells good. What is it?'

'A rabbit,' said Yvonne. 'It was brought here for you, M'sieu, already prepared. They have a great regard for you.'

'And I for them,' said Cris. 'I want you to come into Orléans with us tonight.'

Her eyes lit up.

'*M'sieu!* I was wondering . . .'

She stopped abruptly, for the door opened and Anton came in.

'Le Grisson's all right,' he said. 'He's comfortably bedded down for the day, and Hewison is with him.'

'So Hewey escaped,' I said with relief. 'Thank heaven for that! Isn't he broadcasting?'

'He's going home for a breather,' said Cris, 'but he'll be back. Yvonne, could you collect the bedding in the other hut and get it ready for us to tie on to the car?'

I turned to Anton.

'How is Sheila?' I asked abruptly.

It was absurd, of course, but that was the first time I had mentioned her since seeing Cris and Anton. True, we had not had much opportunity for general conversation, but I had deliberately evaded the subject.

There was a pause, then Cris said: 'She's joined Clyde's staff, Ned.'

'*What!*' I shouted.

Anton gave a comical grimace.

'Shall I tell him, Cris?' Cris nodded, and Anton went on with a relish which I knew was genuine.

It appeared that after Sheila's refusal to visit the Clarices, a family disruption had developed. The trouble, said Anton, was that the Clarices had a son, an eminently suitable young gentleman, and Lady St. Clare undoubtedly thought that Sheila should marry him. Her daughter, however, had other ideas. Lady St. Clare was not a woman one could thwart easily, Anton explained, or, having thwarted and conquered, continue to live with at close quarters. Sheila had therefore used her knowledge of languages to effect, and sought and found a job with Clyde.

I was considerably cheered by what Anton had told me. The effect of it lasted throughout the rabbit stew, which was more than a tribute to Yvonne's ability.

It was about half past three when eventually we left for Orléans, but not before there had been yet another alarm.

17

I Make a Journey by Water

The word of alarm was brought by one of the guerillas, who reached the hut as we were finishing the meal with mugs of coffee.

It appeared that two lorry-loads of *gendarmes* from Orléans with three members of the German Gestapo were on the way to the forest.

'In less than twenty minutes, *M'sieu*, they will arrive. It was not wise for you to make this hut your rendezvous. Paul wishes to know, shall he arrange for them to be ambushed?'

'No,' said Cris sharply. 'We don't want fighting over this. We'll be all right.'

Within ten minutes we were all crowded into the Renault, our bedding tied on to the back. I did not think there was much chance of getting far with it, and expected to have to make our way on foot. Anton, at the wheel, seemed quite contented, however, and started off at a crazy speed along the cart-track.

On what I assumed to be the road to Orléans, we turned right and made for a copse of trees. Here Anton swung off the track with such violence that I thought we would crash. He stopped short, however, with an inch to spare.

A ribbon of road wound below us, and presently we saw a little convoy heading for the forest. A private car led the way, followed by two lorries, crowded with men. Anton laughed aloud.

'There they go, the fools.'

We drove a little way towards Orléans, and then turned right again, on one of the appalling second-class roads. I remember wondering how long a tyre lived under such treatment. Before I had time to dwell on that we climbed a slight rise and then, looking down, saw the wide Loire River.

Presently we turned into the courtyard of a farmhouse which appeared to be empty and derelict; it was. Two scraggy chickens were pecking at the mud, for the warmth of the sun had melted the frost, and the temperature was much higher than it had been in the morning.

'Ah!' exclaimed Anton. 'Our dinner!'

He left the car and started a chase which proved to be a long one, for the fowls finally managed to fly to the roof of the derelict barn, far out of reach of Anton, who stood breathing hard and shaking his fist at them. I think he would have tried to climb to the top, but Cris called him, and he joined us to make the bedding into small bundles, one of which each of us would carry. Cris also carried the oil lamp, and I a tin of paraffin.

Yvonne showed a practicability which cheered me, and some half an hour after we had reached the spot we started to walk down to the nearest hamlet. I felt apprehensive, but had no doubt that Cris knew what he was doing. Yvonne trudged sturdily beside us, with a longer stride than her slight figure led me to expect. She carried her bundle easily, although before long I found mine growing irksomely heavy.

We did not go into the hamlet, it transpired, but stopped at a tiny boathouse on the outskirts. Near it was a sign, reminiscent of good days that seemed lost forever. It declared that boats and punts were for hire, while a regular service ran to Orléans. A written notice pinned to it announced that the boats were no longer for hire, but the ferry-service was maintained.

Out of the hovel next to the boathouse came a shrivelled old woman who eyed us with aversion.

'I've nothing for you here,' she said harshly. 'Nothing.'

Cris said calmly: 'We have come for a boat.'

'A *boat*!' She raised her voice to the high heavens. 'Ask the Boche, go ask them for one of Papa Tivy's boats, and see what they say. A boat! What are you, a fool, a blind man who cannot see that I have no boats?'

Cris took his hand from his pocket; I was surprised to see a little handful of ten-franc notes. The old woman's eyes glittered but she still shook her head, insisting that she had no boat. Cris took his sack from his shoulder and extracted a tin of corned beef. I was watching Madame Tivy, and never has my heart been wrung more than it was then. She did not grab at the tin, but stretched a trembling hand towards it.

Cris gave it to her.

She took it swiftly, hiding it in the folds of her tattered skirt, then without a word she moved to the boathouse and unlocked the iron padlock.

In a few seconds the boat, such as it was, was ours.

I do not know how much Cris paid her; somewhere in the neighbourhood of three hundred francs, I think. He told her that if she inquired at Orléans she might regain the boat, but she must not inquire for a week.

'It is wanted,' he said, 'for *le Liberateur*, Madame Tivy.'

A momentary impression that he had been wrong to use the name faded as she looked at him, and then without speaking pushed the notes into the bow of the boat. She turned and walked away.

Cris picked up a stone and put the notes beneath it, where the old woman could see them when she returned. Then, with Anton and I, he began to push the flat-bottomed tub into the water.

I have perhaps been too disparaging about the boat. It leaked a little, it is true, but Yvonne busied herself with a baling can as soon as we had pushed off. I took the oars. There was ample room for the four of us and although it moved sluggishly, and an occasional eddy carried us perilously near the bank, it was quite riverworthy.

After an hour, when we had travelled perhaps two miles, we ran into a patch of willows overhanging the bank. It was as good a mooring place as any we had passed, and we were hidden from both sides; only river-traffic would come near enough for us to be seen.

It was after dark when we moved off again. I did not enjoy the journey, but the river was wider and there was a moon strong enough for us to see.

We found the mooring place without difficulty, and Anton jumped to the stone quay with one end of a rope which he tied to a ring in the wall. Once we were safely there, and the silence was broken only by the unceasing lapping of the water, I felt the eeriness of it and, perhaps for the first time since I had sighted the village, was worried by a return of my apprehension.

I started violently when a voice came softly from beyond us.

'*I am from Paul*,' a man said.

'*That is quite enough*,' Cris answered.

The rest of the formula was repeated swiftly, and then the man joined us. As I had suspected it was the same one who had warned us to get away from the hut quickly.

'Ned, you and Yvonne stay here, will you?' said Cris. 'We'll be back when we've had a look round.'

I had to make the best of that, although I was a little disgruntled. The others disappeared. As their footsteps faded I realised that I was alone with Yvonne. I felt a little awkward; I am never at my most loquacious with women unless I know them well, when I am apt to talk too much.

Her hand slipped into mine.

'It is cold, Ned.' She had not used my Christian name until then—in fact she had said very little to me, and I was startled. She was certainly cold, but I did not know whether it would be wise to undo one of the bundles of blankets, as there might be the need for hurrying away. So I put an arm about her, and she moved nearer, as a trusting dog might do for warmth. We sat thus in silence for some time, and then she asked me to tell her about Anton.

I realised with a shock that I knew little about him, and was uncertain how much I should say of his recent activities. I confined myself to telling her what I thought were unimportant details, and it seemed to satisfy her. After a while, when she had made no interruption for perhaps five minutes, I stopped and waited for a comment.

Her even breathing was the only response; she was asleep.

I smiled wryly, and wondered what Sheila would think if she could see us. Then my mind worked more freely on Sheila. I thought of her with love and contentment, but it was difficult to fight against sleep. I was getting cramp, too. I had to keep awake, of course, and once I stiffened at the sound of heavy footsteps walking along the cobbles on the river's edge.

A torch shone across the water. Then it went out, and the footsteps drew nearer.

I kept quite still, not waking Yvonne.

The footsteps were so close that I could almost hear the man breathing. Then, just when my own breath was tight within me, he shone the torch again and its beam revealed Yvonne, leaning forward on my shoulder with one arm across my knees.

A ghostly chuckle came from the holder of the torch, which went out; I did not breathe freely for several minutes, while I blessed the sensibilities of the French, their sympathy with love.

His footsteps had almost died away when I heard a rustle on the bank, and then Cris's voice.

'All right, Ned?'

'Yes.' I was too relieved to add anything further. As Cris jumped into the boat Yvonne awakened with a start.

'We've located Vincenne,' Cris said. 'About ten minutes' walk from here. Yvonne, will you mind being by yourself for a while?'

'Of course not.' She sounded a little sleepy although her answer was prompt. 'Will it be safe for me to take out my blanket?'

'Yes,' said Cris, but I sensed that he was dubious. 'Keep the rest of the stuff in a bundle, though, in case we have to move swiftly. Come on, Ned.'

On the way across the cobbles he gave me a brief outline of what we were to do.

Vincenne's house was watched back and front by armed *gendarmes*, neither of whom could be relied on to help us. The house was one in a terrace of tall, narrow buildings, with a good road in front of it and a network of alleys behind, which eventually reached the river. There might be others than Vincenne in the house—by 'others' he meant officials, I gathered—but it was not likely. Paul's men would create a diversion at the front, and if they failed to lure the guard away would put him out of action for at least time enough to enable us to get in the back way, where Anton was waiting and where he would handle the guard. Anton would wait outside while Cris and I went in to overcome any opposition. Vincenne knew of the projected attempt at rescue, and was ready for flight.

'If it's as easy as the le Grisson affair we can't complain,' I said.

'We're in town,' said Cris, rather unnecessarily, I thought. 'If there's an alarm the whole place will be on the lookout for us, and remember our only safe way of escape this time will be by the river.'

'Why is that safe?' I objected.

'Comparatively safe,' corrected Cris. 'We've transport that way. Two miles on the other side of Orléans we've a car waiting. Nobby should arrive, too,' he added.

I was silenced by the information that Nobby Baynes might soon be at hand, and we walked quite openly along the darkened streets. Once the door of an estaminet opened and a couple of men reeled out. One put his arms about me, and I threw him off hurriedly. His companion grew noisily bellicose, and wanted to fight.

Cris snapped at him in a bastard French liberally spattered with German oaths. I have rarely seen a man sober up so quickly. He melted away, dragging his companion with him.

Presently, as we reached an alley leading off the street, Anton loomed out of the shadows.

'All quiet.'

He led us through an open gate. I wondered how he had taken care of his guard. Cris reached the back door and tried the handle. The door opened without difficulty. To me, everything seemed too easy. I had not yet absorbed the fact that the majority of people were our friends, though some, of course, were unwilling to risk letting it be known.

We stepped into an unlighted kitchen.

Through a narrow parlour we went into the main hall. Once there, Cris whistled three times on a low-pitched note. As we waited for a response, a heavy thump sounded above us; at the same time a strangled shout came from outside, followed by running footsteps and what sounded like the muttering of oaths.

'Trouble with the front guard,' Cris said with un-ruffled calm. 'Paul's men will look after him.' He waited until the noise had settled, and then whistled again.

Immediately a light showed from upstairs. An old, rather unsteady voice called:

'A moment, please, and I am ready.'

The light remained; a shadow blocked it for a moment, and then footsteps sounded and the man, presumably Vincenne, began to walk down the stairs. He reached us; he was not so old as I had imagined, and although it was gloomy I thought his face was possessed by fear; dread, perhaps, describes it more accurately. You may have seen the expression in his eyes in paintings of Judas, before he killed himself.

'Cris!' I cried urgently.

'*M'sieu le Liberateur*?' The man's voice quavered; my exclamation had shaken him. I felt in my bones that he had betrayed us. He was trembling; and what was more he had on no outdoor clothes.

Then a door opened and a brighter light flooded the hall, making me close my eyes. But for that I believe I would have flung myself at the men who approached us, four of them all fully armed.

When I did see well enough I knew that one at least was German.

18

In Which I am Subdued by a Story

I had a moment of panic. Vincenne was cringing back against the wall, abject in his treachery, but neither Cris nor I were looking at him.

Then to my stupefaction Cris snarled *in German*.

'What is this? Who are you?' He singled out the German-looking man, whose mouth dropped open. 'What does this mean?' Cris went on in a savage voice, a German voice perfectly imitated. The manner, the arrogance, the spitting gutturals of a Nazi in authority, were all revealed.

The man answered in German. He was an undersized fellow with a face not unlike Goebbels. His collar was too large for him and his Adam's apple moved furiously up and down.

'I do not understand. We came here by arrangement, to arrest . . .' He stopped, swallowed and came out with it: 'The Liberator. We were told he would be calling here.'

'*Ach*, yes,' said Cris. 'You were told! Did you not get my instructions?' He paused, and the man shook his head as if in stupefaction. 'The French swine,' mouthed Cris. 'I sent them. We were to make sure whether Vincenne would try to leave the country, by presenting ourselves as men from the Liberator.'

For a few precious seconds the quartet believed him. One of them stammered out a request to see Cris's authority.

'Authority!' barked Cris. 'God in heaven, do you tell me you have the wit to read?' He dug his hand savagely into his right-hand pocket.

I knew what he was going to do, then. I followed suit, and our guns came out together.

Even then it was touch and go. One man was backing swiftly, and I saw his gun raised. I fired, and he dropped without speaking. I struck the next man a blow which sent him staggering, while Cris had another fellow helpless in a grip which threatened to choke him.

Vincenne, meanwhile, had crumpled in sheer terror to the floor.

Pressing the men back step by step Cris forced them into the room from which they had sprung upon us. He slipped the key from the inside of the door before closing it.

But it was not to be so speedy as that.

There was a thundering knock at the front of the house, while from the streets came the bark of a shot. Paul's men were doing all they could to give us an opportunity for escape. But a bullet broke the glass of the front door, and then a thud followed, suggesting that rifle-butts were being used to break it down. I felt the wind of a bullet as I raced with Cris along the passage to the rear of the house, praying that there was no attack from there.

There was a cold draught coming along the passage; I knew that a door was open. It was lucky for Anton that he spoke before I saw him.

'Hurry, Cris, three or four are coming this way!'

Cris spoke in a rapid undertone.

'Go back for Yvonne, Anton. You've more chance, you haven't been seen. We'll meet you downriver.'

As we reached the alley, windows were being flung up and lights streamed on to the cobbles. It glistened on the trappings of uniforms, and, what was worse, revealed us all too clearly.

'Back into the yard,' Cris snapped.

We heard Anton running, and at least two men after him, but we were too far from him to try to join up, or to include him in our turn-about. We entered the yard and slammed the door in the faces of our nearest pursuers, and then without speaking made for the wall separating Vincenne's garden from the one next door. We must have looked like two jack-in-the-boxes operated by identical springs, for we reached the top of the wall together, put one leg over with almost military precision, paused for a moment to get our balance, and then jumped to the ground.

As we reached the second wall a shot hummed between us; the first climb had been achieved without being noticed, but if we tried the same gambit again we were going to be in trouble.

Already heads and shoulders were showing at the tops of the walls ahead of and behind us, while from the houses with the lights streaming from them came strings of vitriolic curses.

I did not think we should get away.

I believed we would try to get through the house, for that was obviously Cris's intention, but be trapped. I heard myself gasping a protest which was futile, for we had either to go on or be caught, and I knew that further wall-scaling was out of the question.

Then I heard a soft voice say: '*Hurry, hurry, hurry!*'

In French, of course, and so surprising to me that I hesitated in my tracks. Cris did not. He plunged into a scullery like that in Vincenne's house without sparing a glance for the woman who was holding the door open.

The front door also was open, and through this we ran. The crowd in the street had to be seen to be believed; half Orléans must have turned out on the first hint of excitement.

No one tried to impede us, although we were notice-able enough, being the only people travelling away from the scene of the disturbance. No voice, however, and no hand was raised against us.

Breathing heavily, we reached the end of the street and plunged down alleys and side-turnings in an endeavour to reach the river.

Soon we saw lights reflecting on the Loire. A few minutes later we reached the quay. I wondered if Anton had managed to get away.

'Hurry, hurry!' The words came from a white blur, and the voice was Yvonne's.

My elation sobered at once, for I saw that Anton was

in the bottom of the boat and he was not moving.

As we pushed away from the quay there was no sign or sound of pursuit, although the sounds of disturbance reached us from the town itself.

Once in midstream, Cris and Yvonne knelt over Anton. I waited in horror for their verdict.

'Serious?' I gasped at last.

'No,' said Cris, 'I don't think so. It's so confoundedly dark, and I daren't use the torch, but it seems to be a glancing shot in the head.'

That sounded bad enough to me, but apparently Anton was breathing, and there was no immediate need for alarm. I steadied myself and pulled away at the oars.

Slowly, too slowly, the town disappeared behind us. Soon there were fields on either side. It was very quiet. Cris was kneeling in front of me, peering beyond my shoulder. Suddenly he said:

'Easy, Ned.'

I relaxed gladly. The stars were brilliant and it was a glorious night, so that I was able to see much more, now that we were beyond the confines of the city. What I saw startled me: a building, gaunt and forbidding, appeared to frown at me from the south bank.

'There's a turning here,' Cris said. 'A little inlet. Get a bit closer, can you?'

I could, and did. One of my oars scraped against the bank. I manœuvred for position, and then pulled into the mouth of the inlet.

'It's not wide, Ned. There's a jetty over towards the château. Can I give you a breather?'

'Not now,' I grunted. As I had come so far I thought that I might as well finish the job. I wished soon that I had not been so perverse, for it took twenty minutes to find the jetty although I would not let Cris take the oars.

Eventually we grated against stone piles and Cris jumped out, holding the boat close until Yvonne could follow him with the rope. He tied up, then together we lifted Anton, who remained unconscious.

'Where are we?' I asked.

'If Anton were awake he'd tell you!' exclaimed Cris with some emphasis, referring, I supposed, to my interminable questions. I felt a little subdued; Cris was right. On the other hand he need not have snapped so swiftly, I thought.

'Le Château Angriff,' he said a moment later when Anton was lying on the boards of the jetty. 'Any wiser, Ned?'

'Confound you!' I said. 'You know damned well I'm not.'

'How quickly can we get some light, and examine Anton?' demanded Yvonne practically.

'Ned needs a breather,' Cris told her, 'but we won't be long now.' He squatted on his haunches, looking down at Anton and adding: 'It's an old place. Almost a ruin. At least no one can get here without warning us.'

I needed the breather all right, but knew that if I stayed there much longer I would stiffen up, and the task of helping to carry Anton would get much more difficult. So I stood up, and together we carried him along a stony path into the shadows of that gaunt, grim bastion of a past age. The Loire is rich in châteaux; there are dozens, perhaps hundreds of them. And at least one in every three is empty.

After five minutes of walking I realised that we were surrounded by walls. I was about to suggest that we might use the torch when Cris, who had given it to Yvonne, asked her to switch on. The diffused glow showed us the uneven ground, the piles of fallen bricks and stone.

Finally we turned into a small room. I was thankful to see that the roof was still intact.

In a few minutes Cris had the oil lamp out, and was filling it from the carefully stoppered tin of paraffin. He moved Anton into the light, and we were able to see the wound. I was amazed and immensely relieved, for it was no more than a graze running along his temple. The bleeding had been slight, and there was little likelihood of serious consequences.

The discovery cheered us all.

We had a snack from the remains of the rabbit which Yvonne had preserved, with some hard, brown bread which was tasteless and dry. We allowed ourselves a little water from our flask, and then settled down, all three stretched out on blankets spread over the floor. I will not say that it was the acme of comfort, but I was sufficiently at ease to feel rested.

It was a little past nine, and I gathered from Cris that Nobby Baynes would be landing about half a mile from this spot at five o'clock in the morning, so we had ample time to spare.

As we lay there, not yet able to sleep, Cris encouraged Yvonne to talk. She was hesitant at first but gradually gained confidence and lucidity.

Hers was a horrible story, but common enough in those days of horror. She had been the only member of a household of eleven to escape death. Convent trained, gently bred, she had taken to the roads and forests, penniless and alone.

Cris said gently: 'How old are you, Yvonne?'

'Eighteen years and three months,' she said.

I clenched my teeth.

From his corner Anton stirred, and we looked towards

him, making sure that his unconsciousness had now turned to a natural sleep; then Cris said:

'Yvonne, would you rather stay here with us? Or go to England, where you will be quite safe?'

I was surprised, again, that he gave her the choice. The room, if room it could be called, was very silent as she looked at him.

19

In which Nobby Baynes Brings a Warning

I watched the strange smile on Yvonne's lips. Her face was very pale, the shadow cast by the flickering light lying like a sword across her breast.

She spoke slowly: 'I shall not leave France, Cris, while I can give her service.'

I stared at her, astonished.

Cris rose to his feet.

'All right, Yvonne,' he said gently. 'It shall be as you say.'

Nothing else was said; and I was arguing with myself on the wisdom of the decision when a grunt came from Anton's corner.

He opened his eyes, then struggled up to a sitting position. He stared at us wide-eyed, and then Yvonne burst out laughing, while Cris's deep chuckle supplied a bass for her lighter tone. A decidedly lugubrious expression chased stupefaction from Anton's face.

We told him what had happened, and he nodded from time to time, leaning his back against the damp wall of the château. He showed no surprise, and after we had finished he admitted that the only ill-effect he suffered was a headache. There were no other consequences, and he insisted a little later that he could keep watch. He also suggested that we hunt for firewood, but Cris vetoed the suggestion.

'Not until Nobby's been and gone,' he said. 'We don't want anyone to come here while he's about. There isn't much risk of a fire showing, but the smell might attract someone.'

'So be it, I will perish of the cold,' said Anton. 'I am hungry. *Mon Dieu*, am I hungry! Must I starve too?'

He looked at Yvonne, who brought out from her bundle his share of the cold rabbit and the dry bread. None of us was worried about provisions, for Nobby would bring ample supplies.

I took a three-hour stretch of sleep before Anton awakened me. Yvonne and Cris were also sleeping, and we made no sound as we changed places.

As arranged, I awakened Cris at a quarter to five.

The landing-ground, it appeared, was just outside the château, on a flat stretch of meadowland. Cris had the necessary guiding lights and at five minutes past five we heard the faint drone of an aircraft flying high; but for the absolute quiet we would not have heard it.

Cris flashed his torches, white, green and red. The engine appeared to fade away, but after a while we saw the great cross-like shape of the aircraft looming above us. While I knew that a landing in such a situation was not impossible, I stood appalled at the risks which Nobby and his companions ran. They had to do far more than fly over hostile territory and drop their bombs; and I had thought *that* the coolest example of bravery men could show.

This landing in the darkness awed me. Perhaps it was because that gigantic shape, now like a vampire bat, was swooping upon us. I heard the rush of wind past its wings and fuselage.

I shivered, surprised to feel Cris's hand on my shoulder.

'We have to have some light to land in,' he said, 'but the stars are enough most nights. One gets used to it, you know.'

Sane, equable, observant Cris!

He flashed the green light again. Not forty feet from us there was a bump as the wheels touched, and I saw the Battle lurching forward. Cris and I hurried towards it. It was light enough for me to see the shape of Nobby's face, but I could not have identified him with any certainty but for his cheerful voice.

'Any more for the "Skylark"? Don't lose yer chance, ladies. Last trip round the lighthouse before the war starts.'

Crude humour, but heroic. I glowed with admiration for him.

'Hallo, Nobby,' said Cris. 'Ned's here.'

'The Wireless Wizard.' Nobby punched me gently on the chest. 'Ready for a trip back home to ease and comfort?'

'Not yet,' I said.

A member of the crew was bringing out hampers of provisions, paraffin, and first-aid equipment, with other accessories we might need in the next few weeks. Cris had said already that provided we escaped observation Le Château Angriff would be our headquarters.

'No passengers at all?' asked Nobby when we had

finished bringing the goods out. 'All right, Nip, cut along now.'

'You'll want these,' said Cris.

He handed 'Nip', the second pilot, le Grisson's portfolio containing my notes and translations as well as other documents Cris had obtained; the case was sealed and marked for Clyde's attention.

We wished the crew good luck, and then walked towards the château. The violent roar of the engine as the pilot opened the throttle shook the ground, and I was worried lest it be observed and the château visited.

Cris, Nobby and I waited for twenty minutes, straining our eyes for any sign or indication of trouble, but all seemed quiet after the plane's departure.

Back in the room we had commandeered, the lamp was still alight, and Yvonne was sitting near it. Anton lay fast asleep. At sight of Yvonne, Nobby's face registered genuine surprise.

'A new recruit,' Cris told him. 'Yvonne, this is one of our pilots, and he's brought some breakfast.' We put our packages down, Nobby still staring at Yvonne. Before anything else was done, Anton was given the first-aid dressing, long overdue. Yvonne then set about preparing breakfast, while Nobby asked in undertones why the devil we hadn't sent her back to England; there had been plenty of room in the plane.

'She wants to stay, and I think there's plenty for her to do here,' said Cris. 'How long are you staying?'

'Until tomorrow.' Nobby grinned as he lit a cigarette. 'Clyde didn't think the five minutes' wait for the bus to take off again would be enough.'

'Enough for what?'

'Actually I want to check up on one or two landing-grounds near here, but apart from that I've come with an Awful Warning.'

'Thanks,' said Cris. 'What about?'

'Cris, they're after your blood. The Lord knows they wanted Ned badly enough, but over *Le Liberateur* they've started a hue and cry beyond words. Vichy's gone into a panic. The "L" sign is getting as common as the crooked cross.'

'That's a pity,' said Cris thoughtfully. 'If we can't use it safely we'll have to get something else. We'll think about it. Who told you this?'

'Clyde.' The name was enough to make us take the warning seriously. 'The one really up-to-the-minute piece of information, Cris, is that a johnny named Koltz is after you. Our eyes-and-ears-of-the-world boys,' went on Nobby disrespectfully of the Secret Intelligence branch, 'think Koltz a positive wow. Apparently he's been in Poland and Belgium, rooting out the subversive organisations, as Clyde puts it. Koltz is in Vichy now, making arrangements to get hold of you at the same time as he clears up the guerila boys.' Nobby shrugged as he looked round at our sober faces. 'Sorry I'm so grim. I think food might cheer me.' He gazed rapturously at the food Yvonne had laid out, and we sat round it and began to eat. There was coffee from thermos flasks which warmed us and gave me back a courage which had ebbed during Nobby's story. I did not question the details, for I knew how thoroughly the Secret Intelligence worked. It appeared, too, Nobby told us between enormous mouthfuls, that there was a large reward for the apprehension, or knowledge of the whereabouts, of *le Liberateur*.

As he chatted on, I fancied Nobby was perturbed about Yvonne, wondering whether he should talk so freely in front of her. In fact he looked a question at Cris, who smiled reassuringly in return. Yvonne, however, saw the exchange of glances and without a word picked up her share of coffee and sandwiches, and went out.

Nobby spoke swiftly.

'Who is she, Cris? I haven't said too much, have I?'

'No.' Cris was quite definite. He gave a brief résumé of Yvonne's enlistment, and added: 'I think she'll be invaluable although I don't like the idea of using her. She refuses to leave France.'

Anton said seriously: 'I don't like the idea of using Yvonne as a spy.'

'Nonsense,' retorted Cris energetically. 'She's quick-witted, she's burning against the Hun, and it will be a long time before she's suspected of working with us. She'll need grooming, of course. I'd like to keep her here for a week or two, and then send her to London for the grooming. Don't worry about Yvonne,' he added abruptly. 'Koltz is our anxiety at the moment. What else do you know?'

Nobby took a waterproof bag from inside his tunic and handed it to Cris. He opened it, extracting a sealed envelope. The first thing he took out was a photograph.

Have you seen the photographs of von Reichner, who died, they said, of a stroke? A face so hard, so brutal, that it is difficult to believe it is of a human being.

The likeness between Koltz, Ernst Gustav von Koltz as we read in the report Clyde had sent, and the Prussian General was remarkable. The same type, the same brutality.

Cris put the photograph aside, and read the report. It gave us the details of the affairs which von Koltz had conducted, and it told us much of his ruthlessness. It made it clear, also, that Vichy was collaborating with the man to find the Liberator, and enclosed copies of some confidential reports which had found their way out of the hands of Vichy cabinet ministers. I cannot name the minister who passed on that information to us, and continued to help us for a long time until he mysteriously disappeared; we knew, however, that his information was reliable, and Clyde would not have been so definite about von Koltz's new task had he not been absolutely sure.

There is not a lot that I need say of the rest of that day. It began to rain, and very soon a fine drizzle reduced visibility to little more than fifty yards, and any observation of the château so much less likely.

It stood high, as I have said, and no one could approach and take us by surprise; Cris told me that, in clear weather, we could see for twenty miles in every direction.

Cris was very thoughtful all day, and not particularly communicative. Nobby, who was an astute card-player and knew an inexhaustible variety of tricks, intrigued and delighted Yvonne, and then, with Anton and me, initiated her into the mysteries of poker. Some people can play at poker for thirty years and never become accomplished players. Yvonne's mind was quick, and her trick of expressionlessness helped her a great deal.

Throughout the games I found myself wondering whether Cris had not been very wise in letting her stay. I could imagine her developing into a valuable agent; in my bones I knew that she was thoroughly trustworthy.

It was towards evening, when the rain lifted for the first time but visibility remained bad enough for us to know that Nobby would have to stay for the night, that we switched on the portable radio-receiver. Regularly at five o'clock there was a code broadcast for Cris, repeated at six, seven and eight o'clock. I knew the code by heart, as did Cris, but the others were not so well informed. I was able to follow as the announcer read the bulletin,

160

but not until I had it written down did I realise its full meaning.

Already my expression was tense enough to make the others look up eagerly.

The voice stopped, and Anton switched off, demanding:

'What is it, Ned? Another warning?'

'No,' I said. 'No.' I had finished my decyphering before Cris, who put his pencil down and smiled a little grimly.

'Tell 'em, Ned.'

'We've a job all right,' I said slowly, masking my intense excitement, 'von Koltz is in Paris. Clyde thinks there's a chance of our getting him before he gets us.'

20

I Go Again to Paris

Probably the importance of that suggestion to the little party at the château cannot easily be understood. For one thing I think that the effect of Nobby's message had been far greater than I have succeeded in portraying. There was a man-hunt expert on our trail, and we knew that there would be no quarter. Then, Paris was in the heart of occupied France, and was far more dangerous than the zone where we—or at least I—had been operating. Above it all there was the challenge to 'get von Koltz', to smash at the German effort to catch Cris before it had really started.

To me, and I am a man who hesitates to try forlorn ventures, there was a magnificent challenge in the message. I know that Cris and Anton felt pretty much the same, while Nobby leaned back against the wall and whistled the tune of 'It's a long, long way to Tipperary', missing on several notes. The fact that all our preconceived ideas went to the winds meant little; I knew then why Cris always put in the proviso 'If we can' when discussing future operations generally. We had to be prepared for a complete *volte face* at any moment of night or day.

We had spoken in English, but Yvonne understood us. Her eyes were glowing and any lingering doubts I had of her quality disappeared then, for it was clear that she had entered into the affair just as keenly as any of us, and her sense of perception was obviously of a high order.

She broke the ensuing silence.

'Can it be done?' she asked quietly.

'We can try,' Cris said softly. 'My God, we can try! If we can pull it off . . .' He paused. 'Why the devil does it have to happen that we're too far from a transmitter to use one tonight? Anton, are you all right for moving?'

'Yes,' said Anton promptly.

'We must get word through to Paul,' Cris went on. 'We must stop those leaflets appearing in Chartres or Orléans, and concentrate them in Paris. Ned, how well do you know Paris?'

'Nearly as well as I do London,' I told him.

'Good man. You're for Paris, right away. Anton and I will handle Paul. I'll give you one or two addresses,' he added, while silently I wondered how I was going to get to Paris that night, or even the next day. 'Nobby, you'll stay here until further notice, with Yvonne.'

'I have never been to Paris,' said Yvonne musingly.

'You'll be there soon,' said Cris, although I thought that he was a little hesitant. 'We'll come back for you.'

'How do I travel?' I asked.

'By train from Orléans,' said Cris promptly. 'When you've shaved and washed you'll never be recognisable there, and you'll have no trouble.'

He took a notebook from his pocket and scribbled quickly. When he tore out the sheet and handed it to me I read three names and addresses, one in Rue Camembert, one in Rue de l'Opéra, and another in Montmarte, Rue de Cassé. I committed the names and addresses to memory, but tucked the paper into my pocket in case of emergency; on the train I would probably have another opportunity to study them. If, of course, I ever made the train.

'We'll take the boat,' Cris went on, 'and drop you at Orléans, Ned.'

There was a pan of water steaming on the stove, and Cris carried a shaving kit. With the help of a pocket mirror, I shaved for the first time for nearly four days. It proved a tough job, and took me more than a quarter of an hour, but it was done at last.

I thanked the Fates that the rain had stopped, as, with Yvonne and Nobby helping us to get the boat away, we started on the return journey to Orléans.

I suppose the day of inactivity and brooding over von Koltz had numbed my sensibilities, or else I was affected by the burning enthusiasm in Cris and Anton, for I was not apprehensive. Cris was revealing a side to himself that I had rarely seen.

Not until we were in the boat, and I was rowing through the dusk, did I discover what it was.

'Something's bitten you, Cris. What is it?'

'You need ask!' exclaimed Anton. 'He has smelt a German.'

Cris was smiling; I saw that through the gloom.

There was more than a smile on his face, however; there was an expression which I have often seen since. I knew then that Anton was right; Cris had smelt a German. He would go about catching von Koltz with a ruthlessness which would make his earlier rescue efforts seem insignificant. I saw, that night, my first glimpse of the hatred which he felt for all things German; or at least, Nazi.

'Yes,' he said very slowly. 'I don't like working in unoccupied France, Ned. I like to feel that I'm going to send some of the swine to perdition.'

I nodded, and rowed on, not altogether at one with Cris over this, for although I hated them as much as he they failed to inspire in me the same burning, passionate intensity. I knew that was what he was feeling, and I had a strange moment of pity for von Koltz. I shook that nonsense off swiftly, and made good speed. We were going with the tide, and rowing was much easier. Once or twice small craft passed us, and we exchanged comments and bawdy badinage with the occupants, mostly labourers from country districts travelling back from their work.

It was night by the time we reached Orléans. There was more activity by the river quay than there had been the previous night, for we were nearly an hour earlier. We were virtually ignored, however, when we stopped and I handed the oars over to Cris.

On the way he told me that one of the addresses he had given me was of a printer, and I was to have the leaflets printed by the tens of thousand. The printer would arrange for their distribution. At another address, that in Montmartre, I would find our Paris transmitting station. The extent of our preparations in France, in fact, were—and are—far more widespread than many English people dream.

But that will make another story. This is the first of Cris, of the birth of the Liberator and all that he grew to mean in France.

I had promised to destroy the notes before reaching Paris. At the Montmartre rendezvous I would wait for Cris, while the agents I would meet there would get all possible news of von Koltz's movements. The third address, in Rue de l'Opéra, was for emergency, to be used only if I were driven from the others.

I suppose that one of the reasons why I felt quite secure in Orléans was that I had no objective beyond going to the station and catching the first train to Paris. I knew, of course, that the train service would be bad and that it might be twenty-four hours or more before I reached the capital. It was even possible that Cris and Anton would arrive first, but they were to make arrangements with Paul and I did not doubt that there would be some delicate negotiations, for Cris would want everything done his way. He would have to pick men to accompany him, too. I could see in my mind's eye the eagerness with which those men who had driven the *gendarmerie* officers from le Grisson's house would jump at the chance of operating in Paris.

Cris was going to bring six men in all.

I had papers of identity with me, but I knew that there was not a great deal of difficulty in getting into occupied France. The trouble would come in getting out again. But there would be other arrangements made for that. I had no doubt at all that Cris would manage it. My faith in him, perhaps, was more complete than was justified, but time has proved that I was right.

There was a train leaving at ten o'clock for Paris, I discovered, and more than a chance, I was informed with glee, that it would be blown up or wrecked by saboteurs.

This latter knowledge did not add to my ease, but I reasoned that Cris would reach Paul before the train was far out of Orléans, and that any plan to wreck it would be cancelled. I reassured myself with that, at all events, although for the first hour of the journey I was anything but happy. When we stopped with a series of jerks and jolts I was even more apprehensive.

We were only pausing at the 'frontier', however.

German voices echoed about the platform of the wayside station, Germans wrenched open the doors of the carriages and demanded to see our papers.

A bright torch shone on the papers Cris had supplied.

I was Pierre Bedroux, an architect, going to find work in Paris. It was easier, of course, to get in than out, nevertheless I held my breath until my papers were pushed back into my hand.

The journey dragged on interminably. It is about eighty-five miles from Orléans to Paris, and that ride took six hours. What with this, and further time taken for a lengthy re-examination of our papers, the cold light of dawn was already bathing the streets of Paris as I walked out of the Gare d'Orléans.

I was not twenty yards from the station before I saw an old woman washing down a wall on which was chalked: '*Vive le Libérateur!*' The sight elated me, and I stood still for a moment, staring at it.

'Get on, *imbécile*!' hissed the old woman. 'Do you want to spend the night in prison?'

I saw two German soldiers walking on the other side of

the street, and some *gendarmes* looking my way. As I went hurriedly along one of the latter approached me. I went cold with fear lest I had blundered irretrievably and should find myself imprisoned helpless.

The *gendarme* drew alongside me.

'You are fresh into Paris, *M'sieu*?' I did not know whether the quiet tone of his voice meant that he was being friendly or cunning.

'Y-yes,' I stammered, 'I have come to seek work.'

'Work you will find, but not paid for, if you gawk at writings on the wall,' he said. He nodded sagely, and then went on, acknowledging two German N.C.O.s who came along the street. They ignored him. They themselves, I saw, were ignored by all but the *gendarmerie*.

The warning was effective.

I went first to Rue Camembert, and was surprised to find that it was a newspaper office. The paper was one of which I had heard only since the German occupation—*Le Cri*. The man I wanted to see there was named Panneraude.

I need not have worried.

Panneraude was a short, dapper man with a large head, one eye covered with a blue patch. I asked him for work. He told me there was none, and I quoted the watchword: *That is quite enough*.

His one visible eye widened.

We were in a small office which, I gathered, was attached to his living quarters.

He stood up, edging his way to a door opposite that through which I had entered.

'*There cannot be enough until we have reached the end of the road*,' he muttered a little breathlessly.

'*It is not as far as you think*,' I answered.

He led me into another apartment, an untidy living-room which told me that he was a bachelor, and confirmed my first impression that he lived on the premises. As he closed the door he smiled a little.

'You come from him?'

'Yes,' I said. 'Is it all right to talk here?'

'For the moment, yes. Is he aware that von Koltz is in this country, looking for him?'

'He is aware of that, and that von Koltz is in Paris where we want to keep him,' I said swiftly, and then plunged into what Cris had asked me to say.

Panneraude sat back in an uncomfortable-looking chair, his head nodding from time to time. Then his smile widened and he took a pencil from his pocket and scribbled:

> *Vive le Liberateur!*
> *Is he here in Paris?*
> *Is he afraid of von Koltz?*

I frowned.

'I wonder if the second line will warn Koltz that it's a trick,' I said. 'It might seem as if we're trying deliberately to keep him in Paris.'

'Yes.' Panneraude did not dismiss the objection, but insisted: 'He will need to investigate, and when he has found the first rendezvous he wants, he will stay here for others. I think it will serve, *M'sieu*. They will be plastered about Paris during the night, I promise you.'

'Good man,' I said briefly.

He went into another room and brought me some dry, dark bread, and coffee. The coffee was weak, and the wholemeal unpalatable, but I knew that it was the best he had.

We talked fairly generally, and when I had finished, and washed gratefully in a tiny bathroom, he asked whether he would be seeing me again.

'Not in the near future,' I said, 'as far as I know.'

'*Je vous souhaite donc bon voyage, M'sieu.* When you see him, tell him that I am ready, now as always, to do anything I can to help. Tell him'—Panneraude paused—'that he is even more effective than the Voice.'

I was thoughtful as I left him. The absence of taxis made the roads forlorn and deserted.

There were not many Nazis about, although in the Place de la Concorde, with its surround of Government and civic buildings, there were more than in any of the other thoroughfares. Some had fixed bayonets, while a few, obviously on leave, walked about leisurely. There was no single occasion when I saw a German on his own: usually they were in fours or fives, occasionally there were couples.

I saw a cyclist drive straight into a group of five who were crossing to one of the fountains. It could only have been done deliberately. He sent three of them sprawling. and was up on his machine again and off before they collected themselves. No one tried to stop him except a couple of Nazis in the black garb of S.S. men. A crowd impeded them, and they failed with much noisy cursing. Eventually I arrived safely at Montmartre, made my way to Rue de Platte, which I knew well enough, and then asked a little *gamin* for Rue de Cassé. He grinned at me and poked a grimy thumb over his shoulder.

'Down there, *M'sieu*. Be careful!'

Cheeky imp, I thought.

But both his warning and his impudence were justified. In many matters the youth of Paris, particularly in some districts including the Montmarte area, are precocious far beyond their years, and in fact many acted as touts for the brothels with which Rue de Platte was overflowing. There were more red lights over the doorways than I tried to count. I walked as quickly as the cobbles would allow, finally coming to the Rue de Cassé.

It was a broken street with a vengeance!

I am not particularly narrow-minded, but I must confess that my heart dropped when I saw the familiar red bowl above the door of Number 313. Nor was it an encouraging building apart from that. It was one of a dozen houses which looked little more than hovels. A fleshy, red-faced woman sat in the doorway.

'Good morning, *M'sieu*. I can help you?' She was about to begin her patter, but I interrupted swiftly.

'I would like to see *M'sieu* Manet, please.'

'So?' She leered at me and burst into a cackle of laughter. '*M'sieu* Manet, indeed! *M'sieu* Manet! How often they ask for him!' She jumped up from her chair, which creaked noisily, and dived into the dark bowels of the house. She reached the top of a flight of stairs and banged on a door facing them, crying raucously:

'*Madame*, another one!'

Had Cris slipped up?

The door opened.

I suppose the woman who greeted me had once been beautiful. Now she had run to fat. Her luxurious hair was dyed black and she was made up both lavishly and with little thought for detail. She fixed her dark eyes unwinkingly on me.

'*Entrez*,' she commanded.

The room beyond was something like a dressing-room at a third-rate theatre, colourful but tawdry dresses hung from walls, chairs, and on hangers.

She closed the door behind me.

'*Vous venez de lui?*'

The same question which Panneraude had asked; I was

startled by the '*lui*', and by the freedom with which they admitted their knowledge of Cris.

'Yes,' I said. 'I . . .'

'*En voila assez!* She spat at me; I saw suddenly her capacity for venom. I was so startled that it took me a moment to collect myself, but the required formula appeared to satisfy her.

She said abruptly: 'Does he know about von Koltz?'

'Does the whole world know?' I gasped.

'The world that matters, yes,' said *Madame*. 'Sit down, *M'sieu*.' She swept a heap of dresses from a chair. 'What is it you want?'

'I am waiting here for him,' I told her.

'*Nom d'un nom!* In Paris!' She jumped up, her eyes suddenly alight. 'But von Koltz . . .'

'I am only a messenger,' I protested, 'I know little.'

I hoped Cris would not be long, and then went on to ask her to find out all she could about von Koltz.

She was gone for an hour.

When she came back she looked exhausted and was breathing heavily.

'It is known that von Koltz is trying to find us here, *M'sieu*,' she muttered. 'Is it wise for you to stay?'

'Until the last minute, yes,' I said.

She shrugged. 'Word goes round swiftly and you will soon be recognised. I wonder if you are right to stay, *M'sieu*, you in particular.'

I was puzzled. 'Why me, *Madame*?'

'*Nom d'un nom*, your voice!' she spat at me. 'Are you *insane*? The moment I heard you speak I knew it was you.'

I believe that to be an exaggeration; nevertheless, uneasiness is catching, and I soon began to share her apprehension. There was nothing I could do, however, but wait for Cris and Anton.

I stayed in the strange, overcrowded little room until early afternoon. There were two doors to it, one of them concealed behind a wardrobe. Through this the woman led me down a flight of stairs.

A bleak wall with paper peeling from it faced me when I reached the bottom of the stairs; or so I thought. Actually the joins of the paper marked the edges of yet another door, and this she opened by pressing her foot on a piece of wainscotting.

A narrow passage, another door; and then I stepped into a bare, clean room. It was so like the transmitting stations that I had used so often that I stopped on the threshold. It might have been beneath the cottage at Thimert.

Madame clucked her tongue.

'You will be better here. Any messages may come.'

There was no one else present, but I had no need to familiarise myself with the receiving part of the apparatus and put on the earphones. I had had some food, and except that my mind was constantly probing into possibilities concerning Cris, Anton and Yvonne, I was quite content.

There was nothing of importance coming over the air. After a while I took off my earphones and closed my eyes. I must have dozed, for a sharp ring close to me brought me up with a start, and I opened my eyes and stared at the telephone resting on a table close to the wall.

It rang again.

I lifted it, and heard *Madame*'s voice.

'Others will join you,' was all she said, and then rang off.

I was slowly replacing the receiver when Anton and Yvonne, dressed with all the *chic* of a little Parisienne entered.

I stared, looking beyond them for Cris, but he was not there. Quickly Anton gave me a swift résumé of their safe journey into Paris.

It was when I asked about Cris that I realised there was something else on his mind, and for a moment I was filled with alarm.

'Cris is all right,' said Anton quickly.

'Well, what is the matter?' I demanded.

'He wished that he could come here to see you,' said Anton at last. 'But I must talk for him, Ned. Von Koltz remains in Paris because he has heard a rumour that the Voice is in Paris, and will be speaking from here tonight. It was deliberately told to him.'

'What are you driving at?' I demanded.

I could see that he disliked having to tell me something, but for the life of me I could not imagine what it was.

Anton shrugged his shoulders. His eyes were bright, but his smile lacked its usual spontaneity. I was conscious of Yvonne's steady gaze, too, and felt at once apprehensive and irritable. They were at the old game, being mysterious for the sake of it.

'Cris wants you to become yourself again,' said Anton, 'to be seen in the streets before the broadcast, and then to come here. It is considered certain that von Koltz will follow you. He will act himself, he does not delegate important tasks to others, he cannot trust them.'

21

I am the Bait for a Bird of Prey

I sat down heavily in my chair.

Anton seemed more confident now that the message was off his shoulders, and wagged a finger towards me, saying swiftly:

'Some other method can be used, Ned, it is not vital, but it *is* a way in which it can be done. You will see that. Cris asked me not to try to persuade you, or . . .'

'Don't be an oaf,' I said slowly. 'I won't need persuading. The question is, will it work,'

Yvonne exclaimed; it was good to see the way she looked at me, although I was conscious of no heroics, only of a heavy weight of depression as the full demand that was to be made on me became evident. It flashed through my mind that the Voice was a bait which von Koltz would certainly not be able to resist. On the surface the plan had the merit of simplicity, and I did not doubt that Cris would work out the rest with his usual efficiency.

Yet I had to ask whether it would work.

Anton flung up his hands.

'Always the same cautious Ned! Yes, of course it will work. You will be here, von Koltz will come with others. None of them will get away, as we have arranged in other places.'

'As we have . . .' I began, and then remembered abruptly that once discovered, the other places had been blown sky-high. In previous emergencies, however, I had been at a safe distance before the demolition; I saw no way in which I could escape this one.

It is a queer feeling to look ahead and view one's own death.

I took out a cigarette and lit it deliberately.

'I see,' I said. 'Well, the Voice is looked after, now, and my end will make little or no difference.' I drew deeply on the cigarette. 'If von Koltz comes, well and good, but I hope you won't catch a lot of little fishes and lose the big one.'

Anton smiled.

'No, Ned, no. We shall get Koltz. Also, I think, we shall get you away all right, but it was Cris who insisted that I first put it to you like this, so that you could not mistake the risk. It is like him, eh?'

'Yes,' I agreed. 'But there isn't a chance in a thousand of my getting away, and you know it. What time do I broadcast?'

'At half past seven. It is a little after four now. There is a big chance, Ned, but it depends a lot on you. I have been here before, you see, and I know how this works.' He went to the transmitter and put his hand on one of the dials.

Not being a technician, as I have made clear, many of the instruments in the stations were mysteries to me; I handled only those that I needed to know. This one appeared to operate differently, for as he twisted it *the whole apparatus moved slowly from the wall*.

Anton went on before I could speak.

'You need three seconds, Ned, to open that and get up the stairs.' I saw a flight then, beyond the apparatus, leading upwards. 'You need to keep von Koltz and the others occupied for just those three seconds,' Anton went on. 'Tear gas will do it, and not affect you badly if you put on your gas-mask. At the top of the stairs is another door, and when you are through it you will have to get past Koltz's men, but we will be ready to help you there. So'—he looked at me almost pleadingly—'there is a chance, a good one.'

'A magnificent one,' I said sardonically.

And then, for no reason in this wide world, I laughed. The whole set-up struck me as being so incredibly funny that I could not help it. I leaned against the wall and hooted, with Yvonne's eyes open at their widest and Anton staring at me as if I had gone mad; as, I suppose, I had.

I recovered at last and stooped to pick up the cigarette which had dropped from my lips.

'Is he all right?' asked Yvonne.

'God save us, no!' said Anton with feeling. 'No, Yvonne, you and I will never understand him. He is English.'

I remained good-humoured. Indeed, I felt suddenly powerful, as if I could dictate and was in complete command. I often wonder whether I would have felt that way had Cris been present.

'Where are you taking Yvonne, Anton?' I asked.

'To a rendezvous near Versailles,' said Anton promptly. 'When we're through with this she's promised to come to England with us for a month or two.'

'Oh,' I said, for that sobered me abruptly.

With 'us' might be right, but I did not think it likely. I was relieved nevertheless that there was no other dangerous escapade in which Yvonne would be involved.

'We've a landing field on the edge of the Forest of Versailles,' Anton added, 'and we'll be leaving from there tonight.'

'God willing,' I said.

'He will look after you,' Yvonne assured me.

After they had gone I thought a great deal about that remark, but for the time being I was more concerned with arrangements for the bait and the trap. Anton had it all off pat, and I knew that Cris had conceived this scheme and believed that it would succeed.

Once I was free, I was to make for the Place de la Concorde. Opposite l'Hôtel de Ville a car with German officers would be waiting, and I would recognise it by the two men who would be standing by it on the pavement; each with a thumb looped in his belt. It would be a closed car, and inside I could change into German uniform, which would be waiting for me.

'So all I have to do,' I said, 'is to get to the Place de la Concorde. It'll be after dark, I hope.'

'Of course. You will be broadcasting at half past seven, they will trace you soon after that. At the latest, say, half past eight.'

'How am I to be seen and recognised by von Koltz's men?' I demanded.

'*Mon Dieu*! These questions! You will appear in the streets before dark, and then hurry back here. They cannot search the whole of Montmartre in a few minutes, or a few hours. The attention will be centred on Montmartre; the broadcast will make it conclusive. This place will be discovered, Cris has arranged that. Then they will come. Only *Madame* will be here,' he added. 'The place will be empty.'

The 'operation' to turn my chin and eyes back to normal was simple and painless. It took Anton only a few minutes.

'At half past six, or a little earlier, go out,' he admonished me. 'Keep your face hidden as best you can until you are, say, two hundred yards from here. Then show yourself, and come back.'

'That sortie is riddled with risk from the first,' I said gloomily. 'Is there any sense in my going out at all?'

'Cris said so,' declared Anton simply.

I thought of Yvonne and her confident prophecy. *Le Bon Dieu* would see that I escaped. I felt a little guilty of a lack of faith; I suppose I have the average Englishman's faint sheepishness towards religion. I mused on that for some while, and then my mind moved towards Sheila and the possibility of seeing her within twelve hours. Or twenty-four, to make the margin safe.

I laughed suddenly, aloud.

'What a damned fool!' I shouted to the walls. 'What a damned bloody fool! Of course I'll never get away, there isn't a chance in a thousand!'

The sound of my own voice shocked me, and I grew sober. Then I looked at my watch. It was just past six o'clock. There were twenty minutes or a little more before I had to venture out.

The telephone rang at twenty minutes past six.

'Yes?'

Madame's cracked voice answered me.

'I shall come to open the door,' she said, and rang off as abruptly as when she had announced Anton and Yvonne.

I turned my coat collar up, and pulled my shapeless hat well over my eyes.

I saw only *Madame*'s bulky figure and heard only the rustle of her skirts when the door opened and I slipped quickly upstairs, then down the other flight and through the small passage into the light of day.

As I stepped on to the cobbles of the road a man in the black S.S. uniform stared at me, and when I turned left, towards the Rue de Platte, he followed at a slow, careless gait.

22

I Meet Ernst Gustav von Koltz

My heart was palpitating, and I had to force myself to walk
slowly. I was convinced in that moment that Cris was
wrong, and that it had been insanity for me to venture out.
The slow footsteps behind me gave colour to my lack of
faith with every passing second.

The street was by no means empty. There was a
continual hum of conversation as I passed the various
cafés, yet the footsteps of the S.S. guard beat insistently
on my ears; I was conscious of nothing else.

When I reached the Rue de Platte and stopped on a
corner, I hesitated before pushing my hat back and lower-
ing the collar of my coat. I looked along the intersecting
road, but out of the corner of my eye saw the S.S. man.
He approached to within three yards of me, then went
deliberately across the road. He stood on the opposite
corner and stared at me with cold impassiveness.

Then he turned again, and went along the Rue de Platte.

I saw him stop when three men in a similiar uniform to
his own approached him, and for some moments there was
a conference. Then two of the men came in my direction.

How I managed to stand still, and not turn and run, I
do not know. I did stay there, and they sauntered to the
opposite corner and waited, talking idly, looking at me with
covert interest.

Slowly I turned and walked back.

They followed me; again I heard insistent footsteps, two
pairs of feet making them this time instead of one. Oddly

enough, I was now much calmer. It was obvious, I thought, that the man who had first noticed me had gone to report to von Koltz. The others were keeping me in sight, and they would see me go into Number 313.

Sitting on a chair outside the door was the same fleshy red-faced woman who had been there before. She made room for me to pass. I went heavily along the passage and up the stairs, paused and crept down again.

One of the S.S. men was standing on the opposite side of the road. I was quite sure that the other had gone to the back.

It was now nearly a quarter to seven.

I was able to find my own way to the transmitting room. Once inside, I wanted a drink very badly. There was a bottle of cognac and a brandy glass on a tray. I poured a little out, eagerly, draining it off at once. I cannot tell you whether that was good brandy or bad; I know it warmed me, and in a mood of reckless confidence I read the speech which Cris had sent. As I read it I fingered a small glass phial of tear-gas which Anton had left with me.

My ears were cocked to hear any sound of approach, but no one came near me.

I read and re-read the speech until I could have gone to the microphone without the paper and delivered it word-perfect.

In the hour of waiting I smoked six cigarettes, but allowed myself only one other small ration of brandy. I knew that inwardly I was very much afraid. I kept imagining that the door would burst open before I was able to talk, before the arrangements were made for me to make my rush for safety.

At seven-twenty-five I put my watch in front of the broadcasting panel, and tuned in; the movements were mechanical and habitual. I saw the right valves light up, and knew that I was on the air. The second hand of my watch gradually went round twice, and then it was half past seven.

I began to speak:

Citizens of France, tonight I have news for you of first importance. Tonight I can tell you for the first time of the activities here, in Paris, and in other occupied towns and districts of—the Liberator.

I paused, and then went on:

Some of you will have heard of him, some will know that already he is working to free important citizens, men who have courageously waged the war against Hitler, from Hitler's power. For nearly seven weeks now I have given you words of comfort and hope. Now I give you deeds.

I paused again, and then read out a list of names and addresses of the people who had been taken out of France. The last was le Grisson's.

I started on the final paragraph:

Citizens of France! The Liberator is amongst you and will stay amongst you. The Voice is now his Voice, his instrument. You will never be alone, we shall always be with you. Hitler can send his satellites to try to hunt us out, but they will go and we will remain. The day of liberation may be far off; but the sway of the Liberator has begun and will not end until the final liberation.

I finished, staring at the paper, then switched off. I lit another cigarette and took another drink of brandy. I waited for perhaps five minutes, and then cursed myself for thinking that anything could happen so swiftly; I had at least another half an hour to wait.

Actually I had a little more than fifteen minutes.

The first thing I heard was a sharp ring of the telephone, a single jarring note, then silence. With a hand not altogether steady, I held the receiver to my ear. There was a confused shouting, and I knew that orders were being given. I looked at the dial and wondered whether I dared begin my escape, but forced myself to stand by the installation; I must be sure that von Koltz was here.

My teeth were clenched when the door opened suddenly, and I drew back. But it was not von Koltz, only *Madame*, two men thundering down the stairs behind her. I think she would have closed the door but for the human catapult which launched against it; the assault sent her staggering towards me.

After her came two storm troopers, one head first but with a revolver in his hand, the other covering both *Madame* and me.

'Stay where you are!' the man snapped.

I obeyed; I had to obey. I stared tight-lipped at the two men, heard more voices outside, and then a series of quick, firm footsteps.

Von Koltz entered the room.

I recognised him in a flash, and in that moment my thoughts were not of my own plight and of the risks, but of the justification of Cris's contention that von Koltz would come himself.

The hardness of his face was even more apparent in the flesh than it had been in the photograph. He looked more than dissipated; he looked ravaged by some mental disease, as if the evil of Nazi-ism gripped at his vitals and tortured him.

Then von Koltz said: 'So, Deane, we have you at last.'

I said nothing. His voice was grating and metallic, issuing through thin lips barely parted.

'For one who talks so much,' he sneered, 'you are strangely silent. Foolish, too, to allow yourself to be seen leaving and entering this house. *Ach*! You and your voice! And your Liberator! Make no mistake, we will catch him as we have caught you!'

I said slowly: 'You'll never get him, Koltz. I'm not so sure you'll keep me.' I felt uncannily calm, as if I were already dead.

Von Koltz laughed harshly, without merriment.

'You planned to blow this house up, Deane. Very clever, but not quite as clever as I have been.' I tried not to show expression as he spoke, but his words sent a stab of fear through me. His next words made it even worse. 'We knew where this transmitter was, Deane; we have had it cleared of your high explosive.'

I said nothing.

'I came to see you caught with my own eyes,' he went on. 'There is more satisfaction than you can imagine in such a capture. The end of the Voice, the end . . .'

'Oh, no,' I said, and I believe I sounded casual. 'Not the end of the Voice, von Koltz, just the end of mine. There are plenty of others to speak like me. I haven't been broadcasting personally for some time,' I added, and I enjoyed the change of expression on his face—though his eyes remained cold and glassy throughout the whole of that eerie, macabre interview. 'Others have assumed my voice, you see. So simple, Koltz. Hadn't you thought of it?'

'It is a lie!' he rasped.

I laughed at him.

'Oh, Koltz,' I said, 'what a witless fool you are! All that you stand for and all that you've done is shaking now at the beginning of the eruption which will send the lot of you toppling. How can your people have been fooled? How can idiots like you hold sway over them?'

I stopped, and von Koltz barked at me:

'Enough!' He turned to his men. 'Take him.'

Slowly I moved my hand towards the dial, as one of the S.S. men flourished a revolver.

Then I tossed the phial which I had been holding. It struck the peak of von Koltz's hat, and the fragile glass broke immediately. There were three shots, and I heard the bullets crashing into the valves of the apparatus. I remembered that there would be no explosion, while I held my breath as the vapour circled about their heads, affecting them more swiftly than it did me.

The masked door was opening.

Madame thrust something into my hand: a gas-mask. She put hers on, too. The room was filling with people but as they ran into the gas they coughed and choked and were temporarily blinded. I saw that the door was wide enough for us to go through, and I paused a split second for *Madame*; but she pushed me forward with surprising strength, and I raced up the stairs ahead of her, tearing off the respirator as I went.

Madame came behind me.

We reached a landing and what appeared to be a blank wall. *Madame* kicked against a knot in the wainscotting, and a door opened.

Stairs faced us, leading downwards.

I had no time to think, although afterwards I was told that the flight led to the next house. There was another concealed door, and then we burst into a room, a café, in which I drew up sharply; it was filled with grey uniforms!

Three or four rifles were pointed towards us. I was so surprised that I kept quite still; I had believed that Cris would have made some arrangements to let me get into the street.

Then a machine-gun opened fire from across the street. As it began to bark, every German swung towards it. Four of them staggered and were falling as *Madame* pushed me towards the door with a peremptory 'Hurry!'

It looked suicidal.

To go forward was to go into the path of the machine-gun bullets; but there was a chance of a few seconds in which the soldiers might be too busy about themselves to bother about us. I plunged forward. I could not have helped myself in any case, for *Madame* pushed me.

I fully expected to be pitted with bullets.

Instead, the shooting stopped after that one burst, and I reached the door. *Madame* was quickly after me. Immediately the shooting started again.

The street was a long way from empty; grey and black uniforms were everywhere, and I could not conceive how we could possibly get away.

Then *Madame* said: 'Down, Ned, down!'

Again I was pushed forward, but as I sprawled on to the cobbles I was thinking less of our plight and less of von Koltz than of that voice; Cris was there, not *Madame*.

23

I Make Admissions

I had no doubt that the reading of the last few pages seems confusing. It could not be one-tenth as confusing as the actual circumstances were to me. I heard that '*Down, Ned, down*' and recognised Cris's voice, then I was lying full length on the cobbles, hearing the snarl of machine-guns, as bullets pecked at the ground near me.

Then the explosion came; *von Koltz had been wrong.*

Cris had warned me, of course. He must have timed the explosion almost to the second. The blast went over us, but we could hear the tumult of breaking glass and falling debris, the cries of those trapped or wounded. Except for Cris and I, and two men who had been in a café opposite to make the diversion with the machine-gun, no one had expected the explosion.

Thus when we straightened up we were the only men standing. Even ahead of me walls were falling, and glass still tumbling, in a scene of horrible desolation.

The picture of the gap in the houses and the jagged walls on either side is very vivid in my mind, although at the moment the sight hardly registered. Cris was moving fast by then, and despite his skirts he beat me to the first corner. I thought that we would probably be stopped, but had misjudged the stunning effect of the explosion. Yet it was no easy task to push our way through the senseless crowd.

We turned suddenly, Cris leading, into a small café.

The proprietor and his few customers were crowding the

door, but admitted us without question. We hurried along a narrow passage into a smaller room.

There Cris took off the skirt and outer clothes with a speed which surprised me and wiped the paint from his face. The result was not particularly cleansing, but at least it obliterated his past role.

'That'll have to do,' he said. 'We're doing well, Ned.'

'Well!' I echoed.

I could not rid myself of the conviction that the danger was still close upon us. Cris might not be recognised, but I was different. From pegs against the passage wall Cris took a macintosh and I followed his example. There was a hat, too big for me, which I jammed on my head. Even so I felt anything but secure as we left, entering a street which ran parallel to the Rue de Cassé, now thronged with sightseers streaming towards the scene of the explosion.

We walked swiftly, and eventually reached a broader thoroughfare. A fire engine and two ambulances were chasing their way through the narrow streets. By then, however, we had reached a district where the explosion had not caused so devastating an effect, and the people were going in both directions. All the time it was dark and shadowy, except for the moon; looking back, I am surprised that I was so jittery.

Eventually we found a bus.

We sat side by side without joining in the conversation of the others. Like all Paris buses it was crowded, and the passengers jabbered almost entirely about the explosion—not the first and certainly not the last to awaken the city. I gathered that everyone thought that it was sabotage; and there was an undercurrent of jubilation as if the depression which weighted them had lifted for a few precious hours.

We jogged along until we reached the Place de la Concorde.

There was a crowd getting off the bus, but a larger one waiting to take its place. We thrust our way through, and then walked quickly towards the entrance to l'Hôtel de Ville.

A closed car was standing by the kerb. Two S.S. men stood by it, both with their thumbs looped in their belts. We bundled in, the two 'storm troopers' climbed into the front seats. The clutch went in, and we were away.

'And that is the end of von Koltz,' said Cris quietly. 'And a dozen or so others with him, thank God.' His voice held a strange note of harshness as he went on: 'Every one who goes counts, Ned, every one of the swine. I'd like to notch up a hundred thousand.' He paused, then asked: 'What was von Koltz like?'

'His photograph, but ten times worse.'

'Yes,' said Cris. 'They all are. Soulless, inhuman.' We were silent for a while, before he added: 'So it worked out, Ned.'

I admitted that it had worked out far better than I had anticipated, and made several other admissions, including the moments when I had doubted the wisdom of what he had arranged.

'There wasn't any wisdom about it,' he said, in what, for him, was a fairly humble tone. 'It worked, that's the most one can say.' He paused, and then answered my unspoken question. 'I called earlier to see *Madame*, but I hadn't time to come down, Ned. She'd been one of our best people for a long time, but it was getting too dangerous, the house has been suspect for some weeks. We're taking her back to England tonight,' he added. 'Her make-up made it comparatively easy for me to pass myself off. You hadn't twigged it, had you?'

'I had not,' I admitted.

'Good. It's not often one can lay it on with such glorious abandon. We had the two houses on either side emptied, by the way. I doubt whether anyone but the Huns suffered. And they know who did it; there shouldn't be any taking of hostages for this. From tonight onwards we'll be crowding the ether with stories of the Liberator, it will get so deep under the Nazi skin that with luck it will create a permanent irritation.' He added in an oddly serious voice: 'We couldn't have done it without you, Ned.'

'Oh, nonsense!' I said.

'Nonsense if you like, but it's a fact. What did you think of the new Yvonne?'

'You're not leaving her here, are you? Anton said . . .'

'No, we're taking her, but she'll want to come back. And she will. What do you feel about it?'

'Coming back?' I asked.

'Yes.'

'I'm game,' I said, 'for as long as you are.'

He said gruffly: 'Good chap.'

We sped along the road towards Versailles. We were not stopped; the car had some emblem on it which ensured uninterrupted passage, and as he seemed disinclined for further talk I brooded for a while, seeing the glaring flaws in the arrangements, and wondering how it had proved possible for the thing to go through so smoothly.

Finally I asked: 'Cris, why were you so sure that von Koltz would go there in person?'

'He always went everywhere to deliver the *coup de grâce*,' Cris told me. 'His vanity insisted on that.' Cris was harsh-voiced again. 'We'd planted some dynamite in one of the cellars for him to discover, and once that was done he felt quite secure. The transmitter was actually choked with the stuff,' he went on. 'We had four minutes to get up the stairs and into the street; after that we had to take a chance. Two of Paul's men used the machine-gun,' he added slowly. 'I hope they got away; they timed it perfectly.'

I added my fervent hope to his.

Two more of Paul's men, it appeared, had been nearby, ready to lend us a hand had we needed it, while the proprietor of the café where we had earned a temporary respite had been with us, not knowing what was to happen, but prepared to give us sanctuary for as long as we needed it.

Cris's part, of course, loomed largest in my mind at the time, and still does, although when I look at the situation then—and now—dispassionately, I realise that the biggest single contribution to our success, and to the success which we had afterwards, was the ready and self-sacrificing help we obtained from the French people.

Occasionally we had difficulties, as with Vincenne. Once or twice we have been very close to defeat. But now, nearly eighteen months since we left Paris and drove to Versailles, the organisation of *le Liberateur* is far stronger, and more entrenched, then ever.

With the Voice it has not proved difficult to find substitutes, but I am sure that it would be impossible to find a substitute for Cris; he laughs when I say so; but on this, Clyde, Anton and I are fully agreed, and I know Yvonne and others are just as convinced.

We reached the landing-ground in the Forest of Versailles without incident. Anton, Yvonne and Nobby Baynes were waiting for us, with *Madame*—who had been Anton's charge, I learned, since the masquerade had started. Nobby had not been picked up until then, as I have said, because of the weather, but that night was fine and clear. We waited there until the moon was on the wane, then out of the sky came that grotesque, silent, bat-like shape.

We climbed in after a brief exchange of 'How'd-you-do's' with the pilot, and in ten minutes were off.

For some time we said little, then a desultory conversation replaced the quiet; but none of us felt particularly talkative, while *Madame* hardly opened her lips all the way over.

When eventually we landed on the F2 base and she was helped out, I heard her mutter:

'I do not believe it. England! I do not believe it!'

'You'll learn to like it,' said Cris easily.

Madame, I know, is now working with the Free French organisation in England. Of her there is nothing much more I can relate. Of Yvonne, Anton, Cris and I there is a great deal, and I hope to live to tell the story.

I was not thinking of the future that night, however, I was wondering how long it would be before I saw Sheila.

We went to the station commander's office—Cris, of course, had been replaced in view of his more roving commission—and I felt heavy-headed, tired, and very, very dirty.

I saw Clyde; and I saw Sheila.

I forgot the others.

Sheila came towards me, her lovely face holding a message for me which needed no words. I knew when I put my arms about her that I need not have been so careful in my concern for her when I left England; she had committed herself without my help.

My tiredness, my anxieties, my uncertainties, all disappeared. I had no thought for what had happened, only thought for Sheila.

Cris's voice sounded in my ear.

'It's good to know how you two feel,' he said quietly.

'Don't break the news too suddenly to Mother, but between you and me you've Father's full support!'

There was a tap on the door, and Clyde looked in.

'Can you spare five minutes, Cris?' he asked.

'Fifty,' said Cris.

When he had gone, Sheila and I sat on, time forgotten, my awkwardness, my silences, my cautious prophecies, all behind me. Certainly, as we made our plans, we forgot that tomorrow was not ours alone.

If you would like a complete list of Arrow books
please send a postcard to
P.O. Box 29, Douglas, Isle of Man, Great Britain.